Pippi Longstocking

Pippi is nine years old. She lives alone in her own house with a horse and a monkey, and she does exactly as she pleases. She has no mother and she believes her father is the king of a cannibal island. She has never learnt to look after herself and has never been to school. Her friends Tommy and Annika are green with envy—but although they have to go to school and go to bed when they are told, they still have time to join Pippi on all her great adventures.

Astrid Lindgren's stories about Pippi Longstocking are probably her best-known and best-loved. She began her writing career in 1944 after she won a children's book competition. She has published over forty novels for all ages and has won many awards, including the prestigious Hans Christian Andersen Award and The International Book Award.

Pippi Longstocking

Other Oxford Children's Modern Classics

Helen Cresswell
The Piemakers

Gillian Cross
Wolf
The Great Elephant Chase

Nicholas Fisk
A Rag, a Bone and a Hank of Hair

Leon Garfield
Jack Holborn
Mr Corbett's Ghost

Diana Wynne Jones
Cart and Cwidder
Drowned Ammet
The Spellcoats
The Crown of Dalemark

Hilda Lewis
The Ship That Flew

Geraldine McCaughrean
A Little Lower than the Angels
A Pack of Lies

Pat O'Shea
The Hounds of the Morrigan

Philippa Pearce
Minnow on the Say
Tom's Midnight Garden

K. M. Peyton
Flambards
The Edge of the Cloud
Flambards in Summer
Flambards Divided

Rosemary Sutcliff
The Eagle of the Ninth
Outcast
The Silver Branch
The Lantern Bearers

Robert Swindells
Brother in the Land

John Rowe Townsend
Gumble's Yard
The Intruder

Ronald Welch
The Gauntlet

Pippi Longstocking

Astrid Lindgren

Translated by Edna Hurup
Illustrated by Tony Ross

OXFORD
UNIVERSITY PRESS

OXFORD
UNIVERSITY PRESS

Great Clarendon Street, Oxford OX2 6DP

Oxford University Press is a department of the University of Oxford.
It furthers the University's objective of excellence in research, scholarship,
and education by publishing worldwide in

Oxford New York
Athens Auckland Bangkok Bogotá Beunos Aires Calcutta
Cape Town Chennai Dar es Salaam Delhi Florence Hong Kong Istanbul
Karachi Kuala Lumpur Madrid Melbourne Mexico City Mumbai
Nairobi Paris São Paulo Singapore Taipei Tokyo Toronto Warsaw

with associated companies in Berlin Ibadan

Oxford is a registered trade mark of Oxford University Press
in the UK and in certain other countries

British Library Cataloguing in Publication Data available

All foreign and co-production rights shall be handled by Kerstin Kuint Agency AB,
Stockholm, Sweden

ISBN 0 19 271843 6

1 3 5 7 9 10 8 6 4 2

Typeset by AFS Image Setters Ltd, Glasgow
Printed in Great Britain by
Biddles Ltd, Guildford and King's Lynn

Contents

1
Pippi Comes to Villekulla Cottage

AT the end of a little Swedish town lay an old, overgrown orchard. In the orchard was a cottage, and in this cottage lived Pippi Longstocking. She was nine years old, and she lived all alone. She had neither mother nor father, which was really rather nice, for in this way there was no one to tell her to go to bed just when she was having most fun, and no one to make her take cod-liver-oil when she felt like eating peppermints.

There was a time when Pippi had had a father, and she had been very fond of him. Of course, she had had a mother too, but that was long ago.

Pippi's mother had died when Pippi was just a tiny baby lying in her cradle and howling so dreadfully that no one could come near. Pippi believed that her mother now lived somewhere up in Heaven and looked down on her little girl through a hole in it. Pippi often used to wave up to her and say, 'Don't worry, I can look after myself!'

Pippi hadn't forgotten her father. He had been a ship's captain, and sailed on the great ocean. Pippi had sailed with him on his boat, at least until the time he had blown into the sea during a storm and disappeared. But Pippi was quite sure that one day he would come back, for she never believed that he had drowned. She was certain that he had come ashore on a desert island, one with lots and lots of cannibals, and that her father had become king of them all and went about all day with a gold crown on his head.

'*My* father is a Cannibal King; there aren't *many* children with so fine a father!' said Pippi, really pleased with herself. 'And when my father has built himself a boat he'll come to fetch me, and then *I* shall become a Cannibal Princess. What a life it will be!'

Her father had bought the old cottage in the orchard many years ago. He had wanted to live there with Pippi when he grew old and sailed the seas no longer. But then he had unfortunately been blown into the sea, and as Pippi expected him to return she went straight home to Villekulla Cottage, as their house was called. It stood there furnished and ready and waiting for her. One fine summer's evening she had said goodbye to all the sailors on her father's boat. They liked Pippi very much, and Pippi liked them.

'Goodbye, boys!' said Pippi, kissing each in turn on the forehead. 'Don't worry about me. I can take care of myself!'

She took two things from the boat: a little monkey whose name was Mr Nelson (he had been a present from her father) and a big suitcase full of gold pieces. The sailors stood by the rail and watched Pippi until she was out of sight. She kept on walking without turning round once, with Mr Nelson on her shoulder and the suitcase firmly in her hand.

'A remarkable child,' said one of the sailors. wiping a tear from his eye when Pippi disappeared from view.

He was right. Pippi was a very remarkable child, and the most remarkable thing about her was her strength. She was *so* strong that in all the world there was no policeman as strong as she. She could have lifted a whole horse if she had wanted to. And there were times when she *did* want to. Pippi had bought a horse of her very own with one of her gold pieces the day she came home to Villekulla Cottage. She had always longed to have her very own horse, and now there was one living on her front porch. When Pippi wanted to take afternoon tea there, she simply lifted him out into the orchard without further ado.

Next to Villekulla Cottage lay another orchard and another house. In that house lived a mother and a father with their two nice little children, a boy and a girl. The boy's name was Tommy and the girl's Annika. They were both very good and well-brought-up and obedient children. Tommy *never* bit his nails, and *always* did what his mother asked. Annika *never* fussed when she didn't get her own way, and she was always very properly dressed in freshly ironed cotton.

Tommy and Annika played nicely together in their orchard, but they had often wished for a playmate. At the time when Pippi always sailed the seas with her father, they would sometimes hang on the fence and say to each other, 'What a pity no one moves into that house! Someone ought to live there; someone with children.'

The beautiful summer's day that Pippi first crossed the threshold of Villekulla Cottage, Tommy and Annika weren't at home. They were spending the week with their grandmother, and so had no idea that someone had moved into the house next to theirs. The first day after their arrival home they stood by the gate and looked out on the street, and they still didn't know that there was a playmate so near. Just as they stood and wondered what they should do, and if possibly anything *special* would happen that day or if it would be just one of those dull days when one couldn't think of anything in particular to do, why, just then the gate to Villekulla Cottage opened and a little girl appeared. She was the most curious child Tommy and Annika had ever seen. It was Pippi Longstocking going for a morning walk. This is what she looked like:

Her hair was the same colour as a carrot, and was braided in two stiff pigtails that stood straight out from her head. Her nose was the shape of a very small potato, and was dotted with freckles. Under the nose was a really very large mouth, with healthy white teeth. Her dress was curious indeed. Pippi had made it herself. It was supposed to have been blue, but as there hadn't been quite enough blue cloth, Pippi had decided to add little red patches here and there. On her long thin legs she wore long stockings, one brown and the other black. And she had a pair of black shoes which were just twice as long as her feet. Her father had bought them in South America so she would have something to grow into, and Pippi never wanted any others.

The thing that made Tommy and Annika open their eyes widest was the monkey which sat on the strange girl's shoulder. It was little and long-tailed, and dressed in blue trousers, yellow jacket, and a white straw hat.

Pippi went on down the street, walking with one foot on the pavement and the other in the gutter. Tommy and Annika watched her until she was out of sight. In a moment she returned, walking backwards. This was so she shouldn't have to take the trouble to turn round when she went home. When she came level with Tommy and Annika's gate, she stopped. The children looked at each other in silence. At last Tommy said, 'Why are you walking backwards?'

'Why am I walking backwards?' said Pippi. 'This is a free country, isn't it? Can't I walk as I please? Why, let me tell you that in Egypt *everyone* walks that way, and no one thinks it the least bit odd.'

'How do you know that?' asked Tommy. 'You haven't been in Egypt, have you?'

'Have I been to Egypt! You can bet your boots I have. I've been all over the world and seen odder things than people who walk backwards. I wonder what you would have said if I'd walked on my hands like the people do in Indo-China?'

'That can't be true,' protested Tommy.

Pippi considered this for a moment. 'Yes, you're right,' she said sadly, 'I wasn't telling the truth.'

'It's wicked to lie,' said Annika, who at last had found her tongue.

'Yes, it's *very* wicked,' said Pippi, even more sadly. 'But I forget once in a while, you see. How can you expect a little child whose mother is an angel and whose father is a Cannibal King and who has spent her life sailing the seas to tell the truth always? And for that matter,' she said, a smile spreading over her whole freckled face, 'I can tell you that in the Belgian Congo there isn't a single person who tells the truth. They tell fibs all day and every day, begin at seven in the morning and keep it up until sunset. So if I should happen to tell a fib sometimes you must try to forgive me and remember that it's only because I've been a little too long in the Belgian Congo. We can still be friends, can't we?'

'Of course,' said Tommy, realizing suddenly that this *wouldn't* be one of those dull days.

'Why not have breakfast at my house, for that matter?' Pippi wondered.

'Well, yes,' said Tommy, 'why not? Come on, let's!'

'Yes,' said Annika. 'Right away!'

'But first let me introduce you to Mr Nelson,' said Pippi. The monkey raised his hat to them politely.

And so they went through Villekulla Cottage's tumble-down orchard gate and up the path between rows of mossy trees (trees lovely for climbing, they noticed) to the house and on to the porch. There stood the horse, munching oats from a soup tureen.

'Why on earth have you a horse on the front porch?' asked Tommy. All the horses he knew lived in stables.

'Well,' said Pippi after thinking it over, 'he'd be in the way in the kitchen, and he doesn't thrive in the parlour.'

Tommy and Annika patted the horse, and then went on into the house. There was a kitchen and a parlour and a bedroom. But it looked as if Pippi had forgotten to turn out the rooms that week. Tommy and Annika looked carefully about in case that Cannibal King should be in a corner.

They'd never seen a Cannibal King in all their lives. But no father was to be seen, nor any mother, and Annika asked anxiously, 'Do you live here all alone?'

'Of course not,' said Pippi, 'Mr Nelson lives here too.'

'Yes, but haven't you a mother and father here?'

'No, none at all,' said Pippi cheerfully.

'But who tells you when to go to bed at night, and that sort of thing?' asked Annika.

'I do,' said Pippi. 'The first time I say it, I say it in a friendly sort of way, and if I don't listen I say it again more sharply, and if I *still* don't listen, then there's a thrashing to be had, believe me!'

Tommy and Annika didn't quite understand all this, but they thought that perhaps it was a good arrangement. Meanwhile, they had come into the kitchen, and Pippi whooped:

> 'Here pancakes will be baked now,
> Here pancakes will be served now,
> Here pancakes will be fried now!'

At which she took out three eggs and flung them into the air. One of the eggs fell on her head and broke, and the yolk ran down into her eye. But the others she caught properly in a bowl, where they broke.

'I've always heard that egg-yolk is good for the hair,' said Pippi, wiping her eye. 'You'll see that it will grow now so fast it creaks! In Brazil, for that matter, *everyone* goes about with egg in his hair. There's not a bald head to be seen. Once there was an old man who was so odd that he *ate* his eggs instead of spreading them on his hair. He turned quite bald, too, and when he as much as showed himself on the streets the traffic stopped and they had to call out the police.'

While she was talking, Pippi carefully picked out all the broken eggshell from the bowl with her fingers. Then she took a bath-brush which hung on the wall and began beating the batter so that it splattered on the walls. At last she threw what was left on a griddle that stood on the stove. When the pancake was browned on one side she threw it halfway to the ceiling so that it turned in the air and was caught in the pan again. And when it was done, she threw it across the kitchen so that it landed on a plate standing on the table.

'Eat it!' she cried. 'Eat it before it gets cold!'

Tommy and Annika ate, and thought it a very good pancake. Afterwards, Pippi invited them into the parlour. There was only one piece of furniture in it. It was an enormous cupboard with many, many little drawers. Pippi opened them one by one and showed Tommy and Annika all the treasures she kept there. There were strange birds' eggs, and unusual shells and stones, lovely little boxes, beautiful silver mirrors, a pearl necklace, and much more, all bought by Pippi and her father during their travels round the world. Pippi gave her new playmates each a little present as a keepsake. Tommy's was a knife with a gleaming mother-of-pearl handle, and Annika's a little box decorated on the lid with pieces of shell. In the box lay a ring set with a green stone.

'If you should happen to go home now,' said Pippi, 'you'll be able to come again tomorrow. Because if you don't go home, you can't very well come back, and that *would* be a shame.'

Tommy and Annika thought so too, so they went home. They went past the horse, who had eaten up all his oats, and out through the gate of Villekulla Cottage. Mr Nelson waved his hat to them as they left.

2
Pippi is a Turnupstuffer and Gets into a Fight

Annika awoke especially early the next morning. She bounded out of bed and quickly padded over to Tommy.

'Wake up, Tommy!' she said, tugging at his arm. 'Let's go and see that funny girl with the big shoes!'

In an instant, Tommy was wide awake.

'All the time I was sleeping I knew there was going to be something nice about today, though I couldn't remember just what it was,' he said, struggling out of his pyjama-top. Then they both went into the bathroom and washed themselves and brushed their teeth much faster than usual. They were merry and quick about putting on their clothes, and a whole hour earlier than their mother had expected they came sliding down the banister from the top floor and landed exactly by the breakfast table, where they sat down and shouted that they wanted their hot chocolate now, at *once*!

'And may I ask,' said their mother, 'just what it is that makes you in such a hurry?'

'We're going over to see the new girl in the house next door,' said Tommy.

'We might stay all day!' added Annika.

That morning Pippi was baking ginger-snaps. She had made a huge pile of dough, and was rolling it out on the kitchen floor.

''Cause can you imagine,' said Pippi to her little monkey, 'what earthly good a pastry board would be when you're going to make at least five hundred ginger-snaps?'

There she lay on the floor and cut out heart-shaped ginger-snaps as if her life depended on it.

'Do stop walking in the dough, Mr Nelson,' she said irritably just as the doorbell rang.

Pippi ran to open it. She was as white as a miller from top to toe, and when she shook hands heartily with Tommy and Annika a whole cloud of flour came down on them.

'How nice of you to drop in,' she said, shaking a new cloud of flour out of her apron. Tommy and Annika got so much of it in their throats, they had to cough.

'What are you doing?' asked Tommy.

'Well, if I say I'm sweeping the chimney you wouldn't believe me, as clever as you are,' said Pippi. 'As a matter of fact, I'm baking. But that will soon be out of the way. You can sit on the woodbox in the meantime.'

Pippi could work *very* fast. Tommy and Annika sat on the woodbox and watched how she cut her way forward through the dough, and how she threw the biscuits on to the tins, and how she slung the tins into the oven. They thought it was all rather like something in the films.

'All clear,' said Pippi at last, slamming the oven door after the last tins with a bang.

'What are we going to do now?' asked Tommy.

'I don't know what *you're* thinking of doing,' said Pippi, 'but as for me, I'm not one who can take things easy. I happen to be a turnupstuffer, so of course I never have a free moment.'

'What did you say you were?' asked Annika.

'A turnupstuffer.'

'What's that?' asked Tommy.

'Somebody who finds the stuff that turns up if only you look, of course. What else would it be?' said Pippi, sweeping together all the flour on the floor into a little pile. 'The whole world is filled with things that are just waiting for someone to come along and find them, and that's just what a turnupstuffer does.'

'What sort of things?' asked Annika.

'Oh, *all* sorts,' said Pippi. 'Gold nuggets and ostrich feathers and dead mice and rubber bands and tiny little grouse, and *that* kind of thing.'

Tommy and Annika thought it sounded a great deal of fun, and at once wanted to become turnupstuffers too, though Tommy said he hoped he would find a gold nugget and not a little grouse.

'We'll have to wait and see,' said Pippi. 'You always find *something*. But we'll have to hurry up so other turnupstuffers don't come first and take away all the gold nuggets and things that are waiting hereabouts.'

The three turnupstuffers set out. They thought it was best to begin hunting around the houses in the neighbourhood, because Pippi said that even if there *were* little grouse deep in the woods, the *very* best things were almost always found near where people lived.

'Though not always,' she said. 'I've seen it just the other way about. I remember a time when I was looking for things in the jungles of Borneo. Right in the middle of the wild jungle, where no man had ever put his foot, what do you suppose I found? A lovely wooden leg! I gave it away later on to an old man who was one-legged, and he told me that money couldn't buy a wooden leg like that!'

Tommy and Annika watched Pippi to see how a turnupstuffer should act. She ran from one side of the road to the other, shading her eyes with her hand, and searching and searching. Once in a while she crept on her knees, and stuck her hands in through a fence, saying in a disappointed voice, 'Strange! I was *sure* I saw a gold nugget!'

'Can you really take anything you find?' asked Annika.

'Yes, anything that's lying on the ground,' said Pippi.

A little further on, an old man lay sleeping on the lawn in front of his house.

'*That's* lying on the ground,' said Pippi, 'and we've found him. We'll take him!'

Tommy and Annika were horrified.

'No, no, Pippi! We can't take a gentleman! That would never do!' said Tommy. 'Anyway, what would we do with him?'

'What we'd do with him? We could use him for *lots* of things. We could keep him in a little rabbit hutch instead of a rabbit, and feed him dandelion leaves. But if you don't want to, we can leave him here, for all I care. Still, I hate to think that some other turnupstuffer may come along and carry him off.'

They went on. Suddenly, Pippi gave a wild shriek.

'Well, I never saw the likes!' she cried, picking up an old rusty cake tin out of the grass. 'What a find! What a find! One can never have too many tins.'

Tommy looked rather suspiciously at the tin and asked, 'What can you use that for?'

'It can be used for *lots* of things,' said Pippi. 'One way is to put cakes in it. Then it will be one of those nice Tins With Cakes. Another way is *not* to put cakes in it. Then it will be a Tin Without Cakes, which isn't quite as nice, but it would do well enough too.'

She inspected the tin, which really was quite rusty, and had a hole in the bottom.

'It looks as though this one is a Tin Without Cakes,' she said thoughtfully. 'But you can put it over your head and pretend it's the middle of the night!'

And she did just that. With the tin over her

head, she wandered through the neighbourhood like a little tin tower, and she didn't stop before she fell on her stomach over a wire fence. There was a terrific crash when the cake tin hit the ground.

'There, you see!' said Pippi, removing the tin. 'If I hadn't had this on me, I would have fallen face first and knocked myself silly.'

'Yes, but,' said Annika, 'if you hadn't had the tin on you, why, you'd never have tripped over the fence . . . '

But before she had finished speaking, another shriek came from Pippi, who triumphantly held up an empty cotton reel.

'It seems to be my lucky day today!' she said. 'What a perfectly sweet little reel to blow soap bubbles with, or to hang on a string round my neck for a necklace! I want to go home and do it now.'

Just then, the gate to a nearby house opened, and a little boy rushed out. He looked frightened, which wasn't surprising, for hard on his heels came five other boys. They soon got hold of him and pushed him against the fence, where the whole lot attacked him. All five began hitting him at the same time. He cried and tried to shield his face with his arms.

'On him, blokes!' yelled the biggest and the strongest of the boys. 'So he'll never dare show himself in *this* street!'

'Oh!' said Annika. 'That's Willie they're beating. How can they be so horrid!'

'It's that beastly Bengt. He's always fighting,' said Tommy. 'And five against one! What cowards!'

Pippi went up to the boys and tapped Bengt on the back with her finger.

'You there,' she said. 'Do you mean to make pulp of little Willie on the spot, since five of you are at him at once?'

Bengt turned round and saw a girl he'd never met before, an unruly, strange girl who dared to poke him! At first he simply stared in astonishment, and then a broad sneer spread over his face.

'Hey, blokes!' he said. 'Let Willie go, and take a look at this. What a girl!'

He slapped his knees and laughed. In a moment the whole lot had flocked around Pippi. Everyone except Willie, who dried his tears and carefully went and stood beside Tommy.

'Have you ever seen such hair! It's a real flaming bonfire! And what shoes!' Bengt continued. 'Couldn't I please borrow one of them? I'd like to go for a row, and I haven't a boat.'

Then he took hold of one of Pippi's pigtails, but quickly dropped it and said, 'Ouch! I burned myself!'

The five boys made a ring round Pippi and hopped about and yelled, 'Carrot top! Carrot top!'

Pippi stood in the middle of the ring and smiled in a friendly manner. Bengt had hoped she would become angry or begin to cry. At the very least she ought to look scared. When nothing else worked, he pushed her.

'I don't think you have particularly good manners with ladies,' said Pippi. Then she lifted him high into the air with her strong arms. She carried him to a nearby birch tree, and hung him across a branch. Then she took the next boy and hung him on another branch, and then she took the next one and sat him on the high gatepost outside the house, and then she took the *next* one and threw him right over the fence, leaving him sitting in a bed of flowers in the next-door garden. She put the last of the bullies into a little toy cart that stood on the road. Then Pippi and Tommy and Annika and Willie stood looking at the boys a while, and the bullies were quite speechless with astonishment.

Pippi said, 'You are cowards! Five of you go after one boy. That's cowardly. And then you begin to push a little defenceless girl around. Oh, how disgraceful! Nasty!'

'Come on now, let's go home,' she said to Tommy and Annika. And to Willie she said, 'If they try 'n hit you any more, just tell me about it.'

And to Bengt, who sat up in the tree and didn't dare to move, she said, 'If there's anything else you wanted to say about my hair or my shoes, it's best you see to it now, before I go home.'

But Bengt hadn't anything else to say about Pippi's shoes, nor about her hair. And so Pippi took her cake tin in one hand and the cotton reel in the other, and went off, followed by Tommy and Annika.

When they came back to Pippi's orchard, Pippi said, 'Dear hearts, what a shame. Here I've found two such fine things and you haven't found anything at all. You must look a little more. Tommy, why don't you look in that old tree? Old trees are often the very best of places for a turnupstuffer.'

Tommy said that he didn't really think that Annika and he would ever be able to find anything, but in order to please Pippi, he stuck his hand down a hollow in the tree.

21

'Well but—' he said, quite amazed, and pulled out his hand. Between his thumb and forefinger he held a fine notebook with a leather cover. There was a silver pen in a special holder at the side.

'Gosh! That was odd,' said Tommy.

'There, you see!' said Pippi. 'There's nothing better than being a turnupstuffer. It's only a wonder that there aren't more who take up the work. Carpenter and shoemaker and chimney sweep and that sort of thing, *that* they'll become, but turnupstuffer, mark you, that's not good enough!'

And then she said to Annika, 'Why don't you go and feel in that old tree stump? You can just about *always* find things in old tree stumps.'

Annika stuck her hand under the stump, and almost right away got hold of a red coral necklace. Tommy and she just stood and gaped, they were so surprised. They decided that from now on they were going to be turnupstuffers *every* day.

Pippi had been up half the night tossing a ball, so now she suddenly felt sleepy.

'I think I'll go in and have a bit of a snooze,' she said. 'Won't you come along and tuck me in?'

When Pippi sat on the edge of the bed taking off her shoes, she looked thoughtfully at them and said, 'He wanted to go rowing, that Bengt said. Bosh!' she snorted scornfully. 'I'll teach *him* to row, I will! Some other time.'

'I say, Pippi,' said Tommy cautiously, 'why is it you've got such big shoes?'

'Why, so I can wiggle my toes!' she answered. Then she lay down to sleep. She always slept with her feet on the pillow and her head far down under the covers.

'That's the way they sleep in Guatemala,' she explained. 'And it's the only right way to do it. This way, I can wiggle my toes while I'm sleeping, too.

'Can you go to sleep without a lullaby?' she continued. 'I always have to sing to me for a while, else I can't get a wink of sleep.'

Tommy and Annika heard a droning from under the covers. It was Pippi singing herself to sleep. They tiptoed softly out so they shouldn't disturb her. At the door they turned round and took a last look at the bed. They didn't see anything except Pippi's feet on the pillow. There she lay, wiggling her toes energetically.

Tommy and Annika bounded home. Annika clutched her coral necklace tightly in her hand.

'It *was* odd,' she said. 'Tommy, you don't think . . . do you, that Pippi had already put the things there herself?'

'You can't tell,' said Tommy. 'You can't really be certain about *anything* when it comes to Pippi.'

3
Pippi Plays Tag with Policemen

Everyone in the town soon knew that a little girl just nine years old was living alone in Villekulla Cottage. Mothers and fathers shook their heads and agreed that this would not do at *all*. Certainly all children had to have someone to tell them what they ought to do, and all children ought to go to school to learn the multiplication tables. And so they decided that the little girl in Villekulla Cottage should be put into a Children's Home at once.

One beautiful afternoon Pippi had invited Tommy and Annika to her house for tea and ginger-snaps. She set the tea things out on the steps of the front porch. It was sunny and pretty there, and the flowers in Pippi's garden smelled sweetly. Mr Nelson climbed up and down the porch railing, and now and again the horse would stick his nose forward expecting to be offered a ginger-snap.

'How lovely it is to be alive!' said Pippi, stretching her legs out as far as they would go.

Just then two policemen in full uniform came in through the gate.

'Oh!' said Pippi. 'This must be my lucky day, too! Policemen are the very best thing I know. Except for strawberries and cream.'

And she went forward to meet the policemen, her face shining with delight.

'Are you the girl who's moved into Villekulla Cottage?' asked one of the policemen.

'Not me!' said Pippi. 'I'm her very small aunt who lives on the third floor at the other end of the town.'

She only said this because she wanted to have a bit of fun with the policemen. But they didn't think it was the least bit funny. They told her not to try to be so clever. And then they explained that kind people in the town had

26

arranged for her to be placed in a Children's Home.

'I'm already in a Children's Home,' said Pippi.

'What's that? Is it already arranged?' asked the policeman. 'Which Children's Home is that?'

'*This* one,' said Pippi proudly. 'I'm a child, and this is my home. There aren't any grown-ups living here, so I think that makes it a Children's Home.'

'Dear child,' said the policeman, laughing, 'you don't understand. You must come to a regular Institution where someone can look after you.'

'Are horses allowed in the stintitution?' wondered Pippi.

'No, of course not,' said the policeman.

'That's that, I suppose. I thought as much,' said Pippi gloomily. 'Well, how about monkeys, then?'

'Certainly not! I should think you'd know that.'

'I see,' said Pippi. 'Then you'll just have to find yourself kids for that stintitution of yours somewhere else. 'Cause *I* don't mean to move there.'

'Yes, but don't you see, you have to go to school,' said the policeman.

'Why do I?'

'Well, to learn things, of course.'

'What kind of things?' Pippi asked.

'Any number of different kinds,' said the policeman. 'A whole lot of useful things, multiplication tables, for example.'

'I've managed well enough without any pluttification tables for nine years,' said Pippi. 'So I s'pose I can keep managing.'

'Come now! Imagine how unpleasant it will be for you to be so ignorant. Just think, when you grow up and someone perhaps comes and asks you what the capital of Portugal is, you couldn't answer.'

'Oh, yes I could,' said Pippi. 'I'd just say, "If you're all that anxious to know what the capital of Portugal is, well, by all means write direct to Portugal and ask 'em." '

'Yes, but don't you think you'd be sorry you didn't know it yourself?'

'Might be so,' said Pippi. 'I s'pose I *would* lie awake sometimes at night and wonder and wonder, "What the dickens was the name of the capital of Portugal?" But then, you can't have fun *all* the time,' said Pippi, turning a few cartwheels. 'Anyway, I've been in Lisbon with my father,' she continued while upside-down and then right-side-up, for she could talk that way too.

But then one of the policemen said that Pippi shouldn't believe that she could do exactly as she pleased. She would just come along to the Children's Home, and that at *once*. He went towards her and took hold of her arm. But Pippi quickly slipped loose, hit him lightly, and said, 'Tag!' And before he could blink his eyes, she had taken a leap up the post of the porch. With a few pulls she was up on the balcony over the porch. The policemen didn't feel inclined to climb after her the same way, so they rushed into the house and up to the first floor. But when they came out on the balcony, Pippi was already halfway to the roof. She climbed on the roof-tiles very much as if she herself were a monkey. In a moment she stood on the top of the roof and jumped easily up on to the chimney. Down on the balcony both the policemen stood tearing their hair, and on the lawn below stood Tommy and Annika looking up at Pippi.

'What fun it is to play tag!' shouted Pippi. 'And how nice it was of you to come. It's my lucky day today too, that's plain to see.'

When the policemen had thought a moment they went and got a ladder which they leaned against the roof, and then they climbed up, first one and then the other, to fetch Pippi down. But they looked a little bit afraid when they climbed out on to the top of the roof and began balancing their way towards Pippi.

'Don't be scared!' cried Pippi. 'It's not dangerous—just fun!'

When the policemen came within two steps of Pippi, she leaped quickly down from the chimney, and laughing and whooping, ran along the top of the roof to the other gable. A few yards from the house stood a tree.

'Watch me dive!' shouted Pippi, and then she hopped straight down into the tree's green crown, hung fast in a branch, dangled back and forth a moment, and let herself fall to the ground. And then she dashed off on to the other gable and took away the ladder.

The policemen had looked a bit foolish when Pippi jumped, but they looked even more so when they had balanced their way back along the top of the roof and wanted to climb down the ladder. At first they became dreadfully angry and yelled at Pippi, who stood below looking up at them, that she'd better put the ladder back, or else they'd show her a thing or two.

'Why are you so angry?' said Pippi reproachfully. 'We're only playing tag, so we all ought to be friends!'

The policemen thought for a moment, and at last one of them said in a small voice, 'Um, err, I say, wouldn't you be nice and bring the ladder back so that we can get down?'

'Certainly I will,' said Pippi, and brought the ladder back at once. 'And then we can have tea and have a nice time together!'

But the policemen were very deceitful, to be sure, for as soon as they were on the ground they rushed upon Pippi and shouted, 'Now you're going to get it, you nasty child!'

But then Pippi said, 'No, now I haven't time to play any longer. Though it *is* fun, I must admit.'

Then she took a strong hold of their belts, and carried them along the orchard, and out through the gate to the road. There she set them down, and it was a long time before they could bring themselves to move.

'Wait a minute,' shouted Pippi, and ran into the kitchen. She came out with two heart-shaped ginger-snaps. 'Would you like to try one?' she said. 'I don't s'pose it makes much difference if they're a *little* burnt.'

Then she went back to Tommy and Annika, who stood there staring and filled with wonder. And the policemen hurried back to the town and said to all the good mothers and fathers there that Pippi just wasn't quite suitable for a Children's Home. They didn't talk about having been up on the roof. Everyone agreed that perhaps it was best to let Pippi stay in Villekulla Cottage. And if it should happen that she wanted to go to school, then she should arrange that herself.

But Pippi and Tommy and Annika had a really pleasant afternoon. They continued the interrupted tea-party. Pippi gobbled down fourteen ginger-snaps, and then she said, 'Those weren't what I'd call the *best* kind of policemen. No! Altogether too much silly talk about Children's Homes and pluttification and Lisbon.'

Later she lifted out the horse, and then all three of them rode on him. At first Annika was afraid and didn't want to, but when she saw what fun Tommy and Pippi were having she let Pippi lift her up on the horse's back too. And the horse trotted round and round the orchard, and Tommy sang, 'Here come the Swedes with a hullabaloo!'

When Tommy and Annika had crept into their beds that night, Tommy said, 'Annika, don't you think it's jolly that Pippi has moved here?'

'Of course I do,' said Annika.

'I don't even remember what we used to play before she came, do you?'

'Well, we played croquet and *that* sort of thing,' said Annika. 'But somehow it's lots more fun with Pippi, *I* think. And with horses and all that!'

4
Pippi Starts School

Quite naturally, Tommy and Annika went to school. Each morning at eight o'clock they trudged away hand in hand with their school books under their arms.

At that hour Pippi was usually to be found riding her horse or dressing Mr Nelson in his little costume. Or she would be doing her morning exercises, which consisted of standing bolt upright on the floor and then turning forty-three somersaults in the air, one right after the other. After this she would sit on the kitchen table and enjoy a big cup of coffee and a cheese sandwich in peace and quiet.

Tommy and Annika always looked wistfully towards Villekulla Cottage when they toiled away to school. They would much, much rather have gone to play with Pippi. If only Pippi had had to go to school too, it wouldn't have been quite so bad.

'Just think what fun we could have together on our way home from school,' said Tommy.

'Yes, and on the way there too,' Annika agreed.

The more they thought about it, the more it seemed a pity that Pippi didn't go to school. Finally they decided to try and persuade her to begin.

'You can't *imagine* what a nice teacher we have,' said Tommy artfully to Pippi one afternoon when he and Annika were visiting Villekulla Cottage after having first done all their homework.

'Oh, if you *knew* what fun it is at school,' said Annika innocently. 'I should go out of my mind if I couldn't go!'

Pippi sat on a stool washing her feet in a tub. She didn't say anything, but just wiggled her toes a little so the water splashed around.

'One doesn't have to be there so *terribly* long,' continued Tommy. 'Just till two o'clock.'

'Yes, and we get Christmas holidays and Easter holidays and summer holidays,' said Annika.

Pippi bit her big toe thoughtfully, but didn't say anything. Suddenly, without hesitation, she tossed all the water out on the kitchen floor, so that Mr Nelson, who was sitting nearby playing with a mirror, got his trousers absolutely soaked.

'It's unjust!' said Pippi sternly, without taking any notice of Mr Nelson's distress over the wet trousers. 'It's absolutely unjust. I'm not going to stand for it!'

'Not stand for what?' asked Tommy.

'In four months it's Christmas, and you'll be getting Christmas holidays. But me, what do *I* get?' Pippi's voice sounded gloomy. 'No Christmas holidays; not even the very teeniest Christmas holiday,' she complained. 'There's got to be a change here. Tomorrow I'm beginning school!'

Tommy and Annika clapped their hands with joy.

'Hurrah! Then we'll wait for you outside our gate at eight o'clock.'

'No, no,' said Pippi. 'I can't begin *that* early. And for that matter, I think I'll be riding to school.'

And she did. At exactly ten o'clock the next morning she lifted her horse down from the front porch, and a moment later all the people of the little town rushed to their windows to see what horse had run away. That is to say, they *thought* it had run away. But it hadn't. It was simply that Pippi was in a bit of a hurry to get to school. In a wild gallop she burst into the school yard, hopped off the horse at full speed, tied him with a string, and flung open the door of the schoolroom with a terrific crash that made Tommy and Annika and their classmates jump in their seats.

'Hey, hurrah!' shouted Pippi and waved her big hat. 'Am I in time for pluttification?'

Tommy and Annika had explained to their teacher that a new girl called Pippi Longstocking would be coming. The teacher had also heard about Pippi from people in the town. As she was a very kind and pleasant teacher, she had decided to do everything she could to make Pippi feel at home in school.

Pippi flung herself down into an empty seat without anyone having asked her to do so. But the teacher took no notice of her careless manner. She just said in a friendly way, 'Welcome to school, little Pippi. I hope you will be happy here and that you will learn a great deal.'

'To be sure! And *I* hope I'll get Christmas holidays,' said Pippi. ' 'Cause that's the reason I've come. Justice above all things!'

'If you'll first tell me your full name,' said the teacher, 'I shall enrol you in the school.'

'My name is Pippilotta Provisionia Gaberdina Dandeliona Ephraimsdaughter Longstocking, daughter of Captain Ephraim Longstocking, formerly the terror of the seas, now Cannibal King. Pippi is really just my nickname, 'cause my father thought Pippilotta was too long to say.'

'I see,' said the teacher. 'Well then, we shall call you Pippi too. But now perhaps we should test your knowledge a bit,' she continued. 'You're quite a big girl, so you probably know a great deal already. Let us begin with arithmetic. Now, Pippi, can you tell me how much seven and five make?'

Pippi looked rather surprised and cross. Then she said, 'Well, if *you* don't know, don't think I'm going to work it out for you!'

All the children stared in horror at Pippi. The teacher explained to her that she wasn't to answer in that way at school. She wasn't to call the teacher just 'you' either; she was to call the teacher 'ma'am'.

'I'm awful sorry,' said Pippi apologetically. 'I didn't know that. I won't do it again.'

'No, I should hope not,' said the teacher. 'And now I'll tell you that seven and five make twelve.'

'You see!' said Pippi. 'You knew it all the time, so why did you ask, then? Oh, what a blockhead I am! Now I called you just "you" again. 'Scuse me,' she said, giving her ear a powerful pinch.

The teacher decided to pretend that nothing was the matter.

'Now, Pippi, how much do you think eight and four make?'

'I s'pose round about sixty-seven?' said Pippi.

'Not at all,' said the teacher. 'Eight and four make twelve.'

'Now, now, my good woman, that's going too far,' said Pippi. 'You said yourself just now that it was seven and five that made twelve. There oughter be *some* order, even in a school. If you're so keen on this silly stuff, why don't you sit by yourself in a corner and count, and let us be in peace so we can play tag? Oh, dear! Now I said just "you" again,' she said with horror. 'Can you forgive me this last time too? I'll try to remember better from now on.'

The teacher said she would do so. But she thought that trying to teach Pippi any more arithmetic wasn't a good idea. She began to ask the other children instead.

'Can Tommy answer this question, please,' she said. 'If Lisa has seven apples and Axel has nine apples, how many apples have they together?'

'Yes, answer that one, Tommy,' Pippi chimed in. 'And at the same time answer me this one: If Lisa has a tummy ache and Axel has even *more* of a tummy ache, whose fault is it, and where had they pinched the apples?'

The teacher tried to look as if she hadn't heard, and turned to Annika.

'Now, Annika, this problem is for you: Gustav went with his friends on a school outing. He had elevenpence when he went and sevenpence when he came home. How much had he spent?'

'All right,' said Pippi, 'then *I'd* like to know why he was so extravagant, and if it was ginger beer he bought, and if he'd washed well behind his ears before he left home.'

The teacher decided to give up arithmetic completely. She thought that perhaps Pippi would be more interested in learning to read. She therefore brought out a picture of a pretty little green island surrounded by blue water. Just over the island stood the letter 'i'.

'Now, Pippi, I'm going to show you something very interesting,' she said quickly. 'This is a picture of an iiiiiiisland. And this letter above the iiiiiiisland is called "i".'

'Ow, I can hardly believe that,' said Pippi. 'It looks to me like a short line with a fly-speck over it. I'd like to know what islands and fly-specks have to do with each other.'

The teacher brought out the next picture, which was of a snake. She explained to Pippi that the letter over it was called 's'.

'Speaking of snakes,' said Pippi, 'I don't s'pose I'll ever forget the time I fought with a giant snake in India. It was such a horrid snake, you can't *imagine*; he was fourteen yards long and as angry as a bee, and every day he ate up five Indians and two little children for dessert. One day he came and wanted *me* for dessert, and he wound himself round me—krratch—but "I've learned a thing or two at sea," I said and hit him on the head—boom—and then he *hissed*—uiuiuiuiuiuitch—and then I hit him again—boom and—ow—well—then he died. So *that's* the letter "s"? Very interesting!'

Pippi had to catch her breath for a moment. The teacher, who was beginning to think Pippi a noisy and troublesome child, decided to let the class draw for a while. Surely Pippi would sit quietly and draw, thought the teacher. So she brought out paper and pencils and handed them out to the children.

'You may draw whatever you like,' she said,

and she sat down at her desk and began correcting copybooks. After a while she looked up to see how the children were getting on. They all sat looking at Pippi, who lay on the floor drawing to her heart's content.

'But, Pippi,' said the teacher impatiently, 'why don't you draw on the paper?'

'I used that up long ago. There isn't room enough for my whole horse on that silly little scrap of paper,' said Pippi. 'Just now I'm working on the front legs, but when I get to the tail I'll most likely be out in the corridor.'

The teacher thought hard for a moment. 'Perhaps we should sing a little song instead?' she suggested.

All the children stood up beside their seats; all but Pippi, who lay still on the floor.

'Go ahead and sing,' she said. 'I'm going to rest a bit. Too much study can break the healthiest.'

But now the teacher's patience had come to an end. She told all the children to go out into the schoolyard, because she wanted especially to talk to Pippi.

When the teacher and Pippi were alone, Pippi got up and came forward to the desk.

'Do you know,' she said, 'I mean, do you know, *ma'am*, it was really lots of fun to come here and see what it's like. But I don't think I want to go to school any more, Christmas holidays or no Christmas holidays. There's just too many apples and islands and snakes and all that. I just get flustered in the head. I hope you're not disappointed, ma'am.'

But the teacher said she *was* disappointed, most of all because Pippi wouldn't try to behave properly, and that no girl who behaved as badly as Pippi would be allowed to come to school even if she wanted to very much.

'Have I behaved badly?' asked Pippi, very surprised. 'But I didn't know that myself,' she said, looking sad. No one could look as tragic as Pippi when she was unhappy. She stood silently a minute, and then she said in a shaking voice, 'You understand, ma'am, that when your mother is an angel and your father a Cannibal King, and you've travelled all your life on the seas, you don't really know *how* you oughter behave in a school with all the apples and the snakes.'

Then the teacher said that she quite understood, and that she wasn't disappointed in Pippi any longer, and that perhaps Pippi could come back to school when she was a bit older. And Pippi said, beaming with pleasure, 'I think you're awful nice, ma'am. And look what I've got for you, ma'am!'

Out of her pocket Pippi brought a fine little

gold chain, which she laid on the desk. The teacher said she couldn't accept such a valuable gift from Pippi, but then Pippi said, 'You have to! Else I'll come back again tomorrow, and *that* would be a pretty spectacle!'

Then Pippi rushed out into the schoolyard and leaped upon the horse. All the children crowded around to pat the horse and to watch her leave.

'I'm glad I know about Argentine schools,' Pippi said in a superior manner looking down at the children. 'You ought to go *there*! They begin Easter holidays three days after Christmas holidays, and when the Easter holidays are over, it's just three days till summer holidays. Summer holidays are over on the first of November. 'Course, then there's a bit of a grind until Christmas holidays begin on the eleventh of November. But it's not too bad, 'cause at least there aren't any lessons. It's strictly forbidden to have lessons in Argentina. It does happen once in a while that some Argentine child or other hides himself in a cupboard and sits there in secret and reads, but woe betide him if his mother finds him out! They don't have arithmetic in the schools there at all, and if there's a child who knows how much seven and five is, he has to stand in the corner all day if he's so stupid that he tells it to the teacher. They have reading on Fridays only, and then only in case they happen to have some books there. But they never do.'

'Yes, but what do they do in school then?' asked a little boy.

'Eat sweets,' said Pippi without hesitation. 'A long pipe goes direct from a sweets factory in the neighbourhood to the schoolroom. Sweets shoot out of it all day, so the children are kept busy just eating.'

'But what does the teacher do?' asked a little girl.

'Picks the papers off the sweets, dunce,' said Pippi. 'Did you think they did it themselves? Hardly! They don't even as much as go to school themselves. They send their brothers.'

Pippi waved her big hat.

'Yoicks, tally ho!' she cried. 'You won't see me in a minute. But always remember how many apples Axel had, else you'll come to a bad end, hahaha!'

With ringing laughter Pippi rode out through the gate, so fast the gravel whirred around the horse's hooves and the school windows rattled.

5
Pippi Sits on the Gate and
Climbs a Tree

Outside Villekulla Cottage sat Pippi, Tommy, and Annika. Pippi sat on one gatepost, Annika sat on the other gatepost, and Tommy sat on the gate. It was a warm and beautiful day towards the end of August. A pear tree, which grew by the gate, stretched its branches so far down that the children could sit and pick the ripest little yellow-red August pears with no trouble at all. They nibbled and munched, and spat the pear pips out on to the road.

Villekulla Cottage lay just where the little town ended and the countryside began, and where the street turned into a country road. The townspeople liked to go for walks out Villekulla way, for it was there the most beautiful surroundings lay.

While the children sat there eating pears, a girl came by on the road from the town. When she saw the children she stopped and asked, 'Have you seen my father pass by?'

'I don't know,' said Pippi. 'What did he look like? Did he have blue eyes?'

'Yes,' said the girl.

'Black hat and black shoes?'

'Yes, exactly,' said the girl eagerly.

'No, we haven't seen anyone like that,' said Pippi definitely.

The girl looked disappointed and went on without a word.

'Ahoy there!' Pippi shouted after her. 'Was he bald?'

'No, not in the least,' said the girl angrily.

'*That's* a bit of good luck for him!' said Pippi, and spat out a pear pip.

The girl hurried on, but then Pippi yelled, 'Did he have uncommon big ears that reached all the way down to his shoulders?'

'No,' said the girl, and then turned about,

astonished. 'You don't mean to say you've seen a man walk by with ears as big as that?'

'I've never seen anyone walk with his ears,' said Pippi. 'Everybody *I* know walks with his feet.'

'Oof, but you're silly! I mean, have you really seen a man with ears that big?'

'No,' said Pippi. 'There *isn't* anybody with ears that big. Why, that would be absurd. How would it look? One simply can't have such big ears.

'At least, not in *this* country,' she added after a moment's thought. 'In China it's a little different. Once I saw a Chinaman in Shanghai. His ears were *so* big he could use them for a raincoat. When it rained, he just crept in under his ears and was warm and snug as could be. Not that the ears had such a rattling good time of it, you understand. If it was *specially* bad weather, he'd invite friends and acquaintances to pitch camp under his ears too. There they sat, singing their sorrowful songs while it poured down outside. They thought a lot of him because of his ears. Hai Shang was his name. You should have seen Hai Shang running to his work in the morning! He always came charging along at the last minute because he liked sleeping late so much, and you can't imagine how lovely it looked when he came

47

running along with his ears like two big yellow sails behind him.'

The girl had stopped and now stood with open mouth listening to Pippi. And Tommy and Annika had quite forgotten about eating more pears. They were busy enough just listening.

'He had more children than he could count, and the smallest one was called Peter,' said Pippi.

'Yes, but a Chinese child *can't* be called Peter,' objected Tommy.

'That's just what his wife told him too. "A Chinese child *can't* be called Peter," she'd say. But Hai Shang was most *awf'ly* stubborn and he said that the baby would either be called Peter or else nothing at all. And then he sat down in a corner and pulled his ears over his head and just sulked. And so his wife had to give in, of course, and the child was called Peter.'

'Oh, indeed?' said Annika.

'It was the horridest child to be found in all Shanghai,' continued Pippi. 'So fussy with his food, that his mother was quite unhappy. You prob'ly know they eat birds' nests in China? Well, there sat the mother with a whole plateful of bird's nest to feed him. "So, little Peter," she'd say, "now we'll eat a great big bite of bird's nest just for Daddy." But Peter only just clamped his lips together and shook his head. In the end Hai

Shang got so angry that he said no new food should be made for Peter before he'd eaten that bird's nest just for Daddy. And when Hai Shang said a thing, it was *so*. The same bird's nest was sent in and out of the kitchen from May till October. On the fourteenth of July the mother asked couldn't she please give Peter a meat pie, but Hai Shang said no.'

'Nonsense,' said the girl on the road.

'Just what Hai Shang said,' continued Pippi. ' "Nonsense!" he'd say. "There's no reason why a child can't eat bird's nest if he only stops being contrary." But Peter just clamped his lips together the whole time from May till October.'

'Yes, but how could he live, then?' said Tommy in amazement.

'He *couldn't* live,' said Pippi. 'He died. Of contrariness. The eighteenth of October. And buried the nineteenth. And on the twentieth a swallow flew in through the window and laid an egg in the bird's nest that stood on the table. So it didn't go to waste anyway. No harm done!' said Pippi gaily. Then she gazed thoughtfully at the girl who stood in the road looking simply bewildered.

'How odd you look,' said Pippi. 'Just why's that, now? You don't think, do you, that I'm sitting here telling untruths? What's that? Just say so in that case,' threatened Pippi, and rolled up her sleeves.

'No, no, not at all!' said the girl in alarm. 'I wouldn't say you're telling untruths, exactly, but . . .'

'No, no, not at all!' said Pippi. 'But that's just what I *am* doing. I'm telling fibs till my tongue's getting black, can't you see that? Do you really believe a child can live without food from May till October? 'Course, I know well enough they can manage nicely without food three, four months, but from May till October! Why, that's silly! You certainly ought to *know* that's not true. You shouldn't let people make you believe just anything they like.'

Then the girl went her way and didn't once turn around again.

'How simple people can be,' said Pippi to Tommy and Annika. 'From May till October! Why, that's just so *silly*!'

Then she yelled after the girl, 'No, we haven't seen any bald 'uns all day today. But yesterday seventeen of 'em went by. Arm in arm!'

Pippi's orchard was really delightful. It wasn't well looked-after, to be sure, but there were lovely stretches of grass, which were never cut, and old rosebushes full of white and yellow and pink roses. They were not particularly fine roses,

50

perhaps, but sweetly scented. Quite a number of fruit-trees grew there too, and best of all, some old, old oaks and elms which were perfect for climbing.

Climbing-trees were sadly lacking in Tommy and Annika's orchard, and their mother was always rather afraid they would fall down and hurt themselves. For this reason, they hadn't done very much climbing in their day. But now Pippi said:

'What about climbing up in that oak over there?'

Tommy jumped down from the gate at once, delighted with the suggestion. Annika was a little more doubtful, but when she saw there were big bumps on the trunk that one could climb on, she too thought it would be fun to try.

A few yards from the ground the oak divided into two branches, and where it divided it was just like a little room. It wasn't long before all three children sat there. Over their heads the oak spread its crown of leaves like a big green ceiling.

'We could have tea here,' said Pippi. 'I'll pop in and make a drop.'

Tommy and Annika clapped their hands and shouted 'Hooray!'

It wasn't long before Pippi had tea ready. And she'd baked buns the day before. She stood under the oak and began tossing up teacups, and Tommy and Annika caught them. Now and then it was the *oak* that caught them, so that two teacups were broken. But Pippi ran in and fetched new ones. Then it was the buns' turn, and for a long while a cloud of buns whirled in the air. They, at least, didn't get broken. Finally Pippi climbed up with the teapot on her head. She had milk in a bottle in her pocket, and sugar in a little box.

Tommy and Annika thought that tea had never tasted as good before. They weren't allowed to drink tea every day, but only when they were invited out. And now, after all, they *were* invited out. Annika spilled a little tea in her lap; it was warm and wet at first, and then cold and wet, but it didn't matter at all, said Annika.

When they had finished, Pippi flung the cups down to the grass below.

'I want to see how well the china made nowadays wears,' she said. One cup and all three saucers held, strange as it seems. As for the teapot, only the spout broke off.

All of a sudden, Pippi decided to climb a bit higher in the tree.

'Well, I never saw the likes of this before,' she shouted. 'The tree's hollow!'

Going right into the trunk there was a big

hole, which the leaves had hidden from the children's eyes.

'Could I climb up and see too?' said Tommy. But there was no answer. 'Pippi, where are you?' he called uneasily.

Then they heard Pippi's voice, not above them, but far below. It sounded as if it were coming from under the ground.

'I'm inside the tree. It's hollow all the way to the ground. If I peep out through a little crack I can see the teapot on the grass outside.'

'But how are you going to get *up*?' shouted Annika.

'I never can,' said Pippi. 'I'll have to stand here till I get pensioned off. And you'll have to throw food to me through the hole up there. Five, six times a day.'

Annika began to cry.

'But why worry, why complain?' said Pippi. 'Come down here instead, you two. We can play that we're languishing in a dungeon.'

'Not on your life!' said Annika. And for safety's sake, she climbed down out of the tree altogether.

'Annika, I see you through the crack,' shouted Pippi. 'Don't step on the teapot! It's a good old *cosy* teapot that never did a body any harm. And it isn't *its* fault it hasn't a spout any more.'

Annika came up to the tree, and through a little crack she saw the very tip of Pippi's forefinger. This comforted her a great deal, but she was still anxious.

'Pippi, can't you really get up?' she asked.

Pippi's finger disappeared, and in the twinkling of an eye her face popped out through the hole up in the tree.

'Perhaps I can if I really try,' she said, holding the leaves out of the way with her hands.

'Is it that easy to come up?' said Tommy, who was still in the tree. 'Well, then I want to come down and languish a little.'

'Well, first,' said Pippi, 'I think we'll fetch a ladder.'

She crawled out of the hole and slid quickly to the ground. Then she ran to fetch a ladder, struggled with it up the tree, and stuck it down the hole.

Tommy was wildly excited and couldn't wait to go down. It was quite a difficult climb up to the hole as it was rather high, but Tommy was brave. He wasn't afraid to climb into that dark tree-trunk either. Annika saw him disappear, and she wondered if she would ever see him again. She tried to look in through the crack.

'Annika,' she heard Tommy's voice say, 'you can't imagine how wonderful it is here. You must come in too. It's not the least little bit dangerous when you have a ladder to climb on. If you do it just once, you'll never want to do anything else ever.'

'Are you *sure*?' said Annika.

'Absolutely sure,' said Tommy.

So Annika climbed up into the tree again with quaking legs, and Pippi helped her with the last difficult part. She shrank back a little when she saw how dark it was inside the trunk. But Pippi held her hand and encouraged her.

'Don't be afraid, Annika,' she heard Tommy say from inside. 'I can see your legs now, and I'll be sure to catch you if you should fall.'

Annika didn't fall, but came down safe and sound to Tommy. And in a minute, Pippi followed.

'Isn't this spiffing!' said Tommy.

And Annika had to admit that it was. It wasn't nearly as dark as she had thought, because light came in through the crack. Annika went there to make sure that she too could see the teapot on the grass outside.

'We can have this for our hiding-place,' said Tommy. 'Nobody could possibly know we're in here. And if they come round here looking, we can see them through the crack. And *then* we'll laugh!'

'We can have a little stick to poke them with through the crack,' said Pippi. 'Then they'll think there are ghosts.'

With this thought the children became so happy they all three hugged one another. Then they heard the gong-gonging which rang before dinner at Tommy and Annika's home.

'How awful,' said Tommy. 'We have to go home now. But we'll come here tomorrow, as soon as we get home from school.'

'Do,' said Pippi.

So they climbed up the ladder, first Pippi, then Annika, and Tommy after. And then they climbed down the tree, first Pippi, then Annika, and Tommy after.

6

Pippi Arranges a Picnic

'We're having a holiday from school today,' said Tommy to Pippi, ' 'cause it's closed for cleaning.'

'Ha!' cried Pippi. 'Injustice again and again! *I* don't get a holiday, though a bit of cleaning is just what's needed here. Just look at this kitchen floor! But for that matter,' she added, 'when I really think it over, I can clean *without* leave. That's just what I mean to do now, holiday or no holiday. I'd like to see someone try and stop me! If you sit on the kitchen table you won't be in the way.'

Tommy and Annika climbed obediently up on the table, and Mr Nelson jumped up there too and lay down to sleep in Annika's lap.

Pippi warmed a big saucepan of water which she then heaved without ceremony on to the kitchen floor. Then she took off her big shoes and lay them neatly on the breadboard. She tied two scrubbing brushes to her bare feet and then skated over the floor so that it said squish-squeep as she ploughed forward through the water.

'I should have become an ice-skating queen,' she said, lifting one leg high in the air so the scrubbing brush on her left foot knocked a piece off the ceiling lamp.

'Grace and charm I do have, at any rate,' she continued, taking a nimble leap over a chair that stood in her way.

'Well, I should think it's about clean now,' she said at last, taking off the brushes.

'Aren't you going to *dry* the floor?' asked Annika.

'No, it can just vapporpate,' said Pippi. 'I don't s'pose it'll catch cold as long as it keeps moving.'

Tommy and Annika clambered down from the table and stepped across the floor as carefully as they could so as not to get wet.

58

Outside, the sun was shining from a bright blue sky. It was one of those golden September days when one knows it would be lovely to go into the woods. Pippi had an idea.

'What do you think of taking Mr Nelson with us and going on a picnic?'

'Oh, *yes!*' cried Tommy and Annika with glee.

'Run home then, and ask your mother,' said Pippi. 'I'll fix a picnic lunch in the meantime.'

Tommy and Annika thought that it was a fine plan. They rushed home, and it wasn't long before they were back. Pippi was already standing outside the gate with Mr Nelson on her shoulder, a stick in one hand, and a big basket in the other.

At first, the children followed the country road a little way, and then turned off into a field where a pleasant little footpath wound its way between birches and hazel trees. By and by they came to a gate, and past it lay an even lovelier field. But right in front of the gate was a cow, and she didn't look as if she intended to move. Annika shouted at her, and Tommy went bravely forward and tried to shoo her away, but she didn't move an inch, and just stared at the children with her big cow-eyes. To put an end to it all, Pippi laid the basket down, went forward, and lifted the cow away. It lumbered off through the trees in confusion.

'Imagine cows being as pig-headed as that!' said Pippi, jumping with both feet together over the gate. 'And what's the result? The pigs get cow-headed, of course! It's really disgusting to think about it.'

'What a lovely, lovely field!' cried Annika with delight, climbing up on all the rocks she saw. Tommy had taken along his knife, the one he'd got from Pippi, and he cut sticks for both himself and Annika. He cut his thumb a little too, but that didn't matter.

'Perhaps we ought to pick some mushrooms,' said Pippi, breaking off a beautiful red toadstool. 'I wonder if it's eatable,' she continued. 'Anyhow, it certainly isn't *drink*able, that much I know, so there isn't any other choice but to eat it. Perhaps it's all right!'

She bit off a big piece of the toadstool and swallowed it.

'It was!' she pronounced with delight. 'We certainly ought to cook some of these another time,' she said, throwing the toadstool high over the treetops.

'What have you got in the basket, Pippi?' asked Annika. 'Is it anything good?'

'I wouldn't tell you for all the tea in China,' said Pippi. 'First we're going to find a good place where we can set it out.'

The children eagerly began looking for such a place. Annika found a big, flat stone which she thought just right, but it was full of crawling red ants, and 'I shouldn't want to sit down with them, 'cause I don't know them,' said Pippi.

'Yes, and they *bite*,' said Tommy.

'Do they?' said Pippi. 'Bite 'em back, then!'

Then Tommy caught sight of a little glade between two hazel bushes, and that was where he thought they should sit.

'It isn't sunny enough for my freckles to thrive there,' said Pippi. 'And I do think it's nice having freckles.'

A bit further on lay a little cliff which was easily climbed. On the cliff was a sunny little ledge just like a balcony. It was there they sat.

'Now, close your eyes while I set everything out,' said Pippi. Tommy and Annika shut their eyes as tight as they could, and they heard Pippi opening the basket and rustling with paper.

'One, two, nineteen, now you can look!' said Pippi finally. So they looked. And they shouted with delight when they saw all the good things Pippi had set out on the bare rock. There were lovely little sandwiches of meatloaf and ham, a whole pile of pancakes sprinkled with sugar, little brown sausages, and three pineapple puddings.

For, you see, Pippi had learned a great deal from the cook on board her father's ship.

'Gosh, what fun it is to have a holiday!' said Tommy through a mouthful of pancake. 'We ought to have it all the time.'

'No, tell you what,' said Pippi, 'I'm not all *that* fond of cleaning. It's fun, sure enough, but not for *every* day.'

At last the children were so full they could hardly move, and they sat quietly in the sunshine and simply felt good.

'I wonder if it's hard to fly,' said Pippi, looking dreamily over the side of the ledge. The cliff dropped sharply beneath them, and it was far to the ground.

'Going *down* ought to be possible to learn,' she continued. 'It must be *lots* harder going up. But then, one can begin the easy way. I think I'll try!'

'No, Pippi!' cried both Tommy and Annika. 'Oh, dear Pippi, don't do it, please!'

But Pippi already stood at the edge.

'Fly, you flat fly, fly! and the flat fly flew,' she said, and just as she said 'flew', she raised her arms and stepped right into the air. After half a second there was a thud. It was Pippi hitting the ground. Tommy and Annika lay on their stomachs and looked fearfully down at her. Pippi got up and brushed her knees.

'I forgot to flap,' she said easily. 'And I had too many pancakes in me.'

Just at that moment the children discovered that Mr Nelson had disappeared. He had clearly gone off on an outing of his very own. They agreed that they had seen him sitting happily chewing the picnic-basket to pieces, but during Pippi's flying practice they had quite forgotten him. And now he was gone.

Pippi became so angry that she threw one of her shoes into a big, deep pool of water.

'You shouldn't ever take monkeys along when you go somewhere,' she said. 'He should have been left at home to mind the horse. It would have served him right,' she continued, walking into the pool to fetch her shoe. The water reached her waist.

'One should remember to wet the hair, too,' said Pippi, and ducked her head under the water so long it began to bubble.

'There! I won't have to bother about the hair-dresser *this* time,' she continued with satisfaction when she reappeared at last. Then she walked out of the pool and put her shoe on, and they marched off to look for Mr Nelson.

'Listen to the skwuffling when I walk,' laughed Pippi. 'It says "skwuff, skweep" in my clothes, and "skwipp, skwipp" in my shoes. It's funny! I think you should try it too,' she said to Annika, who was walking her pretty way with her fair, silky hair, pink dress, and little white leather shoes.

'Some other time,' said the wise Annika.

They went on.

'I get really angry with Mr Nelson,' said Pippi. 'He does this all the time. He ran away from me once in Sourabaya too, and took a job as a butler with an old widow.

'That isn't true, you know,' she added after a pause.

Tommy suggested that they should each go separate ways to search. Annika was a little afraid and didn't want to at first, but Tommy said, 'You're not a *coward*, are you?'

And of course Annika couldn't stand for that. So all three children went separate ways.

Tommy went across a meadow. He didn't find Mr Nelson, but he *did* find something else. A bull! Or rather, the bull found Tommy, and the bull didn't *like* Tommy, because it was an angry bull who was not in the least fond of children. With a terrible bellow and lowered head he rushed forward, and Tommy let out a wild howl of distress which could be heard through the whole wood. Pippi and Annika heard it too, and came running to see what it was Tommy had meant by his howl. The bull had already caught Tommy on his horns and had tossed him high up in the air.

'What a rude bull!' said Pippi to Annika, who was crying, quite distressed. 'One simply can't act that way. Why, he's dirtying up Tommy's white sailor suit. I'll have to go and talk sense to that stupid bull.'

And she did. She ran forward and pulled his tail.

'Excuse me for interrupting,' she said, and as she was pulling rather hard, the bull turned round and saw a new child which he also wanted to stick with his horns.

'As I said, excuse me for breaking in,' said Pippi again. 'And excuse me for breaking *off*,' she added, and broke off one of the bull's horns. 'It's not fashionable with two horns this year,' she said. 'This year, all the better bulls have only one horn. If any at all,' she added and broke off the other one too.

As bulls have no feeling in their horns, this one didn't know that his were missing. He still tried to butt her, and if it had been anyone but Pippi, there wouldn't have been anything left of that child but apple sauce.

'Hahaha, stop tickling me,' cried Pippi. 'You can't imagine how ticklish I am! Haha, stop, stop, I'll laugh myself to death!'

But the bull didn't stop, and finally Pippi jumped upon his back to get a moment's peace. It wasn't a particularly peaceful place, though, for the bull didn't like having Pippi on his back. He made the very worst sorts of twists and turns to get her off, but she just held tight with her legs and sat where she was. The bull rushed back and forth in the meadow and bellowed so that smoke came out of his nose. Pippi laughed and shouted and waved to Tommy and Annika, who stood at a distance trembling like aspen leaves. The bull turned round and tried to throw Pippi off.

'Look at me dancing with my little friend!' sang Pippi, sitting fast. Finally, the bull became so tired that he lay down on the ground and wished there were no children in the world. For that matter, he had never seen why children were necessary at all.

'Had you thought of taking your afternoon nap now?' asked Pippi politely. 'I shan't disturb you, then.'

She stepped down from his back and went over to Tommy and Annika. Tommy had cried a little. He'd been hurt on one arm, but Annika had wound her handkerchief round it, so it didn't hurt any longer.

'Oh, *Pippi*!' cried Annika, full of excitement when Pippi came.

'Ssh!' whispered Pippi. 'Don't wake the bull! He's sleeping, and if we wake him he'll just be cross.

'Mr Nelson! Mr Nelson! Where are you?' she shouted the next minute in a shrill voice without bothering about the bull's afternoon nap. 'We have to go home!'

And indeed, there sat Mr Nelson huddled up in a pine tree. He was chewing his tail, and looked very unhappy. It wasn't much fun for such a little monkey to be left alone in the woods. Now he hopped down from the pine tree and up on Pippi's shoulder, and he waved his straw hat as he always did when he was especially happy.

'So you didn't become a butler this time,' said Pippi stroking his back. 'Bosh, *that* was a true fib,' she added. 'But if it was true, how could it be a fib? Perhaps when all's said and done, he really *has* been a butler in Sourabaya, after all! Well, if that's so, I know who's going to serve dinner from now on!'

And so they wandered home, Pippi still in dripping clothes and squelching shoes. Tommy and Annika thought they had had a wonderful day, except for the bull, and they sang a song they had learned at school. It was really a summer song, and now it was almost autumn, but they thought it would do just the same.

'When summer days are warm and still
We like to go o'er wood and hill
Let the journey be as hard as it will,
We'll sing as we go, Hi ho, hi ho!
All children, hear!
Join us and sing,
O, make the air with music ring!
Our happy band will never stop,
We'll keep on climbing up, up, up,
Until we've reached the very top!
When summer days are warm and still,
We sing as we go, Hi ho, hi ho!'

Pippi sang too, but she didn't use quite the same words. She sang like this:

'When summer days are warm and still
And I go over wood and hill
I do exactly what I will
And it drips as I go, Hi ho, hi ho!
And in my shoes,
Because I choose,
It squelches just like orange juice
Because the shoes are soaking wet.
Ho, ha, what a silly bull we met!
And I—I do like chicken croquette!
When summer days are warm and still
It drips as I go. Drip ho! drip ho!'

7
Pippi Goes to the Circus

A circus had come to the little town, and all the children ran to their mothers and fathers and begged to be allowed to go. Tommy and Annika did so too, and their kind father at once gave them some of the shiny Swedish silver coins called crowns.

With their money held tightly in their hands, they rushed over to Pippi. She was on the front porch with the horse, arranging his tail into small braids, each tied with a red ribbon.

'Today is his birthday, I think,' she said, 'so he has to be dressed up.'

'Pippi,' said Tommy, panting, for they had run so fast, 'Pippi, can you come with us to the circus?'

'I can do anything I please,' said Pippi, 'but I don't know if I can come to the sarcus, 'cause I don't know what a sarcus is. Does it hurt?'

'How silly you are!' said Tommy. 'It doesn't hurt! It's just fun! Horses and clowns and beautiful ladies who walk on a rope!'

'But it costs money,' said Annika, opening her little hand to see if her three shiny crowns still lay there.

'I'm rich as a goblin,' said Pippi, 'so I suppose I can always buy a sarcus. It's going to be crowded if I have any more horses, though. The clowns and those beautiful ladies could squeeze into the laundry-house, but it's more of a problem with the horses.'

'What nonsense!' said Tommy. 'You're not going to *buy* the circus. It costs money to go there and look, don't you see?'

'Heaven help me!' cried Pippi, shutting her eyes tight. 'Does it cost money to *look*? And here I've been going around with my eyes open all day and every day! Goodness knows how much money I've used up already!'

Then little by little she carefully opened one eye, and rolled it round and round in her head. 'Cost what it will,' she said, 'I must have a peep now!'

Tommy and Annika finally succeeded in explaining to Pippi what a circus was, and then Pippi went and took some gold pieces out of her suitcase. After that she put on her hat, which was as big as a mill-wheel, and they started off for the circus.

There was a crowd of people outside the circus tent, and in front of the ticket window stood a long queue. By and by it was Pippi's turn. She stuck her head through the window, looked hard at the dear old lady who sat there, and said, 'How much does it cost to look at *you*?'

The old lady was from a foreign country, so she didn't understand what Pippi meant. She answered, 'Liddle girl, it is costink vive crones the front rows and dree crones the back rows and wan crones the zdandinkroom.'

'I see,' said Pippi. 'But you must promise that you'll walk on the rope too.'

Now Tommy stepped in and said that Pippi would have a ticket for the back rows. Pippi gave a gold piece to the old lady, and she looked suspiciously at it. She bit it, too, to see if it were real. At last she was convinced that it really was gold, and Pippi got her ticket. She got a great many silver coins in change as well.

'What do I want with all that nasty little white money?' said Pippi crossly. 'Keep it. I'll look at you twice instead. From the zdandinkroom.'

So, as Pippi absolutely didn't want any money back, the lady changed her ticket for a front row one, and gave Tommy and Annika front row tickets as well, without their having to add any money of their own. In this way, Pippi and Tommy and Annika came to sit on some very fine red chairs by the ringside. Tommy and Annika turned round several times in order to wave to their schoolmates, who sat much further away.

'*This* is a queer hut,' said Pippi, looking about her with wonder. 'But they've spilled sawdust on the floor, I see. Not that I'm fussy, but it *does* look a bit untidy.'

Tommy explained to Pippi that there was always sawdust in circus rings for the horses to run on.

On a platform sat the circus musicians, and they suddenly began to play a rousing march. Pippi clapped her hands wildly and jumped up and down in her chair with delight.

'Does it cost something to listen, too, or can you do that free?' she wondered.

Just then the curtain was pulled back from the artistes' entrance, and the ringmaster, dressed in black and with a whip in his hand, came running in, and with him there came ten white horses with red plumes on their heads.

The ringmaster cracked his whip, and the horses cantered round the ring. Then he cracked his whip again, and they all stood with their front legs up on the railing which circled the ring. One of the horses had stopped just in front of the children. Annika didn't like having a horse so close to her, so she crouched back in her chair as far as she could. But Pippi leaned forward, lifted up the horse's front leg, and said, 'How's yourself? My horse sends his regards to you. It's *his* birthday too today, though he has bows on his tail instead of his head.'

As luck would have it, Pippi let go of the horse's foot before the ringmaster cracked his whip the next time, because then all the horses jumped down from the railing and began to canter again.

When the act was finished, the ringmaster bowed beautifully, and the horses trotted out. A second later the curtain opened again for a coal-black horse, and on his back stood a beautiful lady dressed in green silk tights. Her name was Miss Carmencita, it said in the programme.

The horse trotted round in the sawdust, and Miss Carmencita stood there calmly and smiled. But then something happened. Just as the horse passed Pippi's place, something came whistling through the air. It was none other than Pippi herself. There she suddenly stood on the horse's back behind Miss Carmencita. At first, Miss Carmencita was so astonished that she nearly fell off the horse. Then she became angry. She began to hit behind herself with her hands in order to get Pippi to jump off. But she couldn't manage it.

'Calm down a little,' said Pippi. 'You're not the only one who's going to have fun. There are others who've paid *their* money too, believe it or not!'

Then Miss Carmencita wanted to jump off herself, but she couldn't do that either, for Pippi had a steady hold round her waist. The people in the circus couldn't help laughing. It looked so silly, they thought, to see the beautiful Miss Carmencita held fast by a little red-headed scamp who stood on the horse's back in her big shoes looking as if she'd never done anything *but* perform in a circus.

But the ringmaster didn't laugh. He made a sign to his red-coated attendants to run forward and stop the horse.

'Is the act over already?' said Pippi, disappointed. 'Just now when we were having such fun!'

'Derrible child,' hissed the ringmaster between his teeth, 'go avay!'

Pippi looked sorrowfully at him. 'Well, but, now,' she said, 'why are you so angry with me? I thought everyone was supposed to have a nice time here.'

She jumped down from the horse, and went and sat down in her place. But now two big attendants came to throw her out. They took hold of her and tried to lift her.

It was no use. Pippi just sat still, and it simply wasn't possible to move her from the spot, though they tugged as hard as they could. So they shrugged their shoulders and went away.

In the meantime the next act had begun. It was Miss Elvira, who was to walk the tightrope. She wore a pink tulle dress and carried a pink parasol in her hand. With small neat steps she ran out on to the rope. She swung her legs and did all manner of tricks. It was very pretty indeed. She proved too that she could go backwards on the thin rope. But when she came back to the little platform at the end of the line and turned round, Pippi was standing there.

'What was it you said?' said Pippi, delighted to see Miss Elvira's surprised expression.

Miss Elvira didn't say anything at all, but jumped down from the rope and threw her arms around the neck of the ringmaster, who was her father. Again he sent for his attendants to throw Pippi out. This time he sent for five. But all the people in the circus shouted, 'Let her be! We want to see the little red-head!'

And they stamped their feet and clapped their hands.

Pippi ran out on the line. And Miss Elvira's tricks were nothing compared to what Pippi could do. When she came to the middle of the rope, she stretched one leg straight up into the air, and her big shoe spread out like a roof over her head. She waggled her foot a little, to scratch behind her ear.

The ringmaster was not the least bit pleased that Pippi was performing in his circus. He wanted to be rid of her. So he sneaked forward and loosened the mechanism which held the line tight, and he was sure that Pippi would fall off.

But she didn't. She began to swing the rope instead. Back and forth swayed the line, faster and faster swung Pippi, and then—suddenly—she took a leap into the air and landed right on the ringmaster. He was so frightened that he began to run.

'This horse is even more fun,' said Pippi. 'But why haven't you any tassels in your hair?'

Now Pippi thought it was time to turn back to Tommy and Annika. She climbed off the ringmaster and went and sat down, and then the next act was about to begin. There was a moment's delay, because the ringmaster first had to go out and drink a glass of water and comb his hair. But after that he came in, bowed to the audience, and said, 'Ladies and chantlemen! In ze next moment you vill zee vun of ze vunders uff all time, ze zdrongest man in ze vorld, Mighty Adolf, who nobody has effer beaten yet. And here he is, ladies and chantlemen. Mighty Adolf!'

A gigantic man stepped into the ring. He was dressed in scarlet tights, and he had a leopard skin round his stomach. He bowed to the audience, and looked very self-satisfied indeed.

'Just *look* at which mossels!' said the ringmaster, squeezing Mighty Adolf's arm where the muscles bulged like bowls under the skin.

'And now, ladies and chantlemen, I giff you a grrreat offer! Weech of you dares to try a wrestling match with Mighty Adolf, who dares to try to beat ze vorld's zdrongest man? A hundred crowns I pay to the vun who can beat Mighty Adolf. A hundred crowns, consider it, ladies and chantlemen! Step right up! Who'll giff it a try?'

Nobody came forward.

'What did he say?' asked Pippi. 'And why is he speaking Arabian?'

'He said that the person who can beat that great big man over there will get a hundred crowns,' said Tommy.

'I can do it,' said Pippi. 'But I think it would be a shame to beat him, 'cause he looks such a nice man.'

'But you could *never* do it,' said Annika. 'Why, that's the strongest man in the world!'

'Man, yes,' said Pippi. 'But I'm the strongest *girl* in the world, don't forget.'

In the meanwhile, Mighty Adolf was lifting dumb-bells and bending thick iron bars to show how strong he was.

'Now, now, goot people!' shouted the ringmaster. 'Is there rilly nobody who should like to vin a hundred crowns? Must I rilly keep them for myself?' he said, waving a hundred-crown note.

'No, I rilly don't think you must,' said Pippi, climbing over the railing to the ring.

'Go! Disappear! I don't vant I should zee you,' the ringmaster hissed.

'Why are you always so unfriendly?' said Pippi reproachfully. 'I only want to fight with Mighty Adolf.'

'Zis is no time for chokes,' said the ringmaster. 'Go avay, before Mighty Adolf hears your impertinence!'

But Pippi went right past the ringmaster and over to Mighty Adolf. She took his big hand in hers and shook it heartily.

'Now, shall we have a bit of a wrestle, you and I?' she said.

Mighty Adolf looked at her and didn't understand a thing.

'In one minute I'm going to begin,' said Pippi.

And she did. She grappled properly with Mighty Adolf, and before anyone knew how it had happened, she'd laid him flat on the mat. Mighty Adolf scrambled up, quite red in the face.

'Hurrah for Pippi!' shouted Tommy and Annika. All the people at the circus heard this, and so they shouted, 'Hurrah for Pippi!' too. The ringmaster sat on the railing and wrung his hands. He was angry. But Mighty Adolf was angrier still. Never in his life had anything so terrible happened to him. But now he would show this little red-haired girl what kind of a man Mighty Adolf was! He rushed forward and took a strong grip on her, but Pippi stood as fast as a rock.

'You can do better than that,' she said to encourage him. Then she prised herself free from his grip, and in a second, Mighty Adolf was lying on the mat again. Pippi stood beside him and waited. She didn't have to wait long. With a bellow he raised himself and stormed at her again.

'Tiddlelipom and poddeliday,' said Pippi.

All the people at the circus stamped their feet and threw their caps up in the air, and shouted, 'Hurrah for Pippi!'

The third time Mighty Adolf rushed at her, Pippi lifted him high into the air and carried him on her upstretched arms around the ring. After that, she laid him on the mat and held him there.

'Now, my boy, I think we've had enough of this sort of game,' she said. 'It won't get any more fun than this, anyway.'

'Pippi is the winner! Pippi is the winner!' shouted all the people at the circus. Mighty Adolf slunk out as fast as he could. And the ringmaster had to go forward and present Pippi with the hundred-crown note, though he looked as if he would rather have eaten her up.

'Here you are, my young lady, here is your hundred crowns!'

'That?' said Pippi scornfully. 'What should I do with that piece of paper? You can have it to wrap fish in, if you want!'

Then she went back to her place.

'This is a long-lasting circus, this one,' she said to Tommy and Annika. 'Forty winks might not do any harm. But wake me if there's anything else I need to help with.'

So she lay back in her chair and went to sleep immediately. There she lay snoring while clowns and sword-swallowers and snake-people showed their tricks to Tommy and Annika and all the other people at the circus.

'Somehow, I think Pippi was best of all,' whispered Tommy to Annika.

8
Pippi is Visited by Thieves

After Pippi's performance at the circus there
was not a person in the little town
who didn't know how fearfully strong
she was. There had even been articles about
her in the newspaper. But people who lived
elsewhere naturally didn't know who Pippi
was.

One dark autumn night two tramps came
wandering by on the road past Villekulla Cottage.
They were two nasty, shabby thieves who had set
out through the countryside in order to see if

they could find something to steal. When they saw that there was a light on in Villekulla Cottage, they decided to go in and ask for a sandwich.

That evening Pippi had emptied out all her gold pieces on the kitchen floor and sat counting them. She wasn't very good at counting, to be sure, but she did it anyway once in a while. Just to keep things in order.

' . . . seventy-five, seventy-six, seventy-seven, seventy-eight, seventy-nine, seventy-ten, seventy-eleven, seventy-twelve, seventy-seventeen, pooh! There must be other numbers to be had. 'Course, now I remember! One hundred and four, a thousand. Bless be! *that's* a lot of money!' said Pippi.

Just then there was a knock at the door.

'Come in or stay where you are, just as you like,' yelled Pippi. 'It's not for me to decide!'

The door opened and the two tramps came in. You can be sure their eyes grew big when they saw a little red-haired girl sitting there quite alone on the floor counting money.

'Are you at home all alone?' they asked craftily.

'Not at all,' said Pippi. 'Mr Nelson is at home too.'

The thieves couldn't very well know that Mr Nelson was just a little monkey who lay sleeping in his green-painted bed with a doll's blanket round his stomach. They thought it was the man of the house whose name was Mr Nelson, and they winked slyly at each other.

'We can come back a little later,' they meant with that wink, but to Pippi they said, 'Well, we just came in to see what your clock says.'

'Big, strong fellows who don't know what a clock says!' said Pippi. 'What kind of bringing up did you have? It says tick tock. Now I suppose you'll want to know what it does? Well, it goes and goes and never comes to the door. If you know any more riddles, just come along with them,' she said encouragingly.

The tramps thought that Pippi was probably too little to understand about clocks, so they turned and went out again without a word.

'Holy mackerel! Did you see all that money?' said one.

'What a piece of luck,' said the other. 'All we have to do now is wait until the little girl and that Nelson fellow are asleep. Then we can slip in and lay our hands on the whole lot.'

They sat down under an oak tree in the orchard to wait. A cold drizzle fell and they were very hungry. It was really quite unpleasant, but the thought of all that money kept them in good spirits.

In all the other houses, the lights went out one by one, but in Villekulla Cottage they still kept on burning. For Pippi was busy teaching herself to dance the polka, and she didn't want to go to bed before she was sure she knew how. Finally, though, the windows of Villekulla Cottage became dark as well.

The tramps waited a good while so as to be certain that Mr Nelson would be asleep. At last they sneaked forward to the back door and got ready to open it with their house-breaking tools. One of them (his name was Bloom, by the way) in the meantime tried the door by pure accident. It wasn't locked.

'They must be out of their heads!' he whispered to his comrade. 'The door's wide open!'

'So much the better for us,' answered the comrade, a dark-haired fellow called Thunder Karlson by those who knew him.

Thunder Karlson lit his torch, and then they sneaked into the kitchen. There was nobody there. In the next room was Pippi's bed, and there, too, was Mr Nelson's little doll's-bed.

Thunder Karlson opened the door and carefully looked in. It was peaceful and still, and he let the flashing light of the torch play around the room. When the stream of light fell on Pippi's bed, both the tramps saw, to their astonishment, nothing but a pair of feet resting on the pillow. As usual, Pippi had her head under the covers down at the foot of the bed.

'That must be the little girl,' whispered Thunder Karlson to Bloom. 'And she's certainly asleep. But where d'you think Nelson is?'

'*Mr* Nelson, if you don't mind,' came Pippi's calm voice from under the covers. 'Mr Nelson is lying in that little green doll's-bed.'

The tramps were so alarmed that they were about to rush out at once. But then they thought over what Pippi had said. *Mr Nelson lay in the doll's-bed!* By the light of the torch they could see the doll's-bed and the little monkey who lay in it. Thunder Karlson couldn't help laughing.

'Bloom,' he said, 'Mr Nelson is a monkey, hahaha!'

'Well, what did you think he was?' came the calm voice from under the covers. 'A lawnmower?'

'Aren't your mother and father home?' asked Bloom.

'No,' said Pippi. 'They're gone. Quite gone!'

Thunder Karlson and Bloom chuckled with joy.

'Well, little lady,' said Thunder Karlson, 'come out, we'd like to talk to you.'

'No, I'm asleep,' said Pippi. 'Was it something

about clocks again? 'Cause in that case, can you guess what kind of a clock . . . '

But before she could finish, Bloom took a firm hold of the covers and pulled them off Pippi.

'Can you dance the polka?' asked Pippi, looking him solemnly in the eyes. '*I* can!'

'You ask so many questions,' said Thunder Karlson. 'Can we ask some too? For example, where have you got the money you had on the floor?'

'In the suitcase there on the cupboard,' Pippi answered truthfully.

Thunder Karlson and Bloom grinned.

'I hope you don't mind me taking it back, little friend?' said Thunder Karlson.

'Oh, not at all,' said Pippi. ' '*Course* not!'

Whereupon he went over and lifted down the suitcase.

'I hope you don't mind me taking it back, little friend?' said Pippi, climbing out of bed and padding over to Bloom.

Bloom didn't know just how it happened, but the suitcase was suddenly in Pippi's hand.

'This is no joke,' said Thunder Karlson angrily. 'Give us that suitcase!'

He grabbed Pippi hard by the arm and tried to snatch away the much-desired prize.

'*I* wasn't joking,' said Pippi, lifting up Thunder Karlson and putting him up on the

87

cupboard. A minute later Bloom sat there too. Then the tramps both became frightened. They began to understand that Pippi was not exactly an ordinary girl. But they wanted the suitcase so much that they forgot their fears.

'All together, Bloom!' cried Thunder Karlson, and they jumped down from the cupboard and hurled themselves on Pippi, who held the suitcase in her hand. But Pippi poked them with her forefinger so that they sat down hard each in a corner. Before they were able to get up, Pippi had got out a rope, and as quick as thought she bound fast the arms and legs of both the thieves. Now they changed their tune.

'Kind, good little missie,' begged Thunder Karlson, 'forgive us, we were only joking! Don't hurt us, we're just two poor penniless tramps who came in to ask for a bit of food.'

Bloom even shed a tear or two.

Pippi put the suitcase in its proper place on the cupboard. Then she turned to her captives.

'Can either of you dance the polka?'

'Well, brrumph, that is . . . ' said Thunder Karlson. 'I should think we've both done a bit along that line.'

'Oh, what fun!' said Pippi, clapping her hands. 'Couldn't we give it a try? I've just learned how, you see.'

'Yes, by all means!' said Thunder Karlson, somewhat bewildered.

Then Pippi took a big pair of scissors and cut the ropes that bound her guests.

'Oh, but we haven't any music,' said Pippi sorrowfully. Then she had an idea.

'Couldn't you play on the comb,' she said to Bloom, 'while I dance with him?' She pointed to Thunder Karlson.

Why, yes. Bloom would certainly play the comb. And he did, so that it could be heard all over the house. Mr Nelson was startled out of his sleep and sat up in his bed just in time to see Pippi whirling about with Thunder Karlson. She was dreadfully serious, and she danced with great energy as if her life depended on it.

At the end, Bloom didn't want to play on the comb any longer, as he claimed it tickled his mouth unmercifully. And Thunder Karlson, who had been trudging along the road all day long, began to have tired legs.

'Just a little while longer,' begged Pippi, and continued dancing. There was nothing for Bloom and Thunder Karlson to do but continue too.

When it was three o'clock in the morning, Pippi said, 'Oh, I could keep on till Thursday! But perhaps you're tired and hungry?'

And that was just what they were, though they hardly dared to say so. Pippi brought out bread and cheese and butter and ham and cold steak and milk from the cupboard, and then they sat round the kitchen table, Bloom and Thunder Karlson and Pippi, and ate until they were just about square. Pippi tossed a little milk into one of her ears.

'It's good for earache,' she said.

'What a shame! Have you an earache?' said Bloom.

'No,' said Pippi. 'But I might get one!'

Finally the two tramps got up, thanked Pippi very much for the food, and asked might they please say goodbye now.

'How nice it was that you came! Must you really go so soon?' Pippi complained.

'Never have I seen anyone who could dance the polka like you, my little honey-bun!' she said to Thunder Karlson.

'Practise hard at playing on the comb,' she said to Bloom, 'then you won't feel it tickle any more.'

Just as they got to the doorway, Pippi came running and gave them each a gold piece.

'You've honestly earned this,' she said.

9
Pippi Goes to a Tea Party

Tommy and Annika's mother had invited some ladies to a tea party, and as she had baked so very many cakes she decided to let Tommy and Annika invite Pippi at the same time. In this way, she thought, she wouldn't have any bother with her own children.

Tommy and Annika were overjoyed when they were told this, and they ran straight away over to Pippi to invite her. Pippi was walking about in her orchard watering the few poor remaining flowers with an old, rusty watering-can. As it was pouring with rain that day, Tommy told Pippi he thought it was really rather unnecessary.

'That's all very well for *you* to say,' said Pippi indignantly. 'But I lay awake all night looking forward to getting up and watering the flowers. You can bet your boots I'm not going to let a little rain stop me!'

Now Annika came out with the wonderful news about the tea party.

'Tea party . . . *me?*' cried Pippi, becoming so nervous that she began to water Tommy instead of the rosebush in question. 'Oh, what will happen? Help! I'm so nervous! What if I can't behave myself?'

'Why, *'course* you can,' said Annika.

'Don't be too sure about that,' said Pippi. 'I do try, believe me, but I've noticed lots of times that people don't think I'm behaving even though I've really truly tried to just as nicely as ever I could. At sea we never did fuss much with such things. But I promise I'll put my shoulder to the wheel good and proper today so you won't have to be ashamed of me.'

'Fine,' said Tommy, and then he and Annika dashed home again through the rain.

'This afternoon at three, don't forget!' shouted Annika, looking out from under the umbrella.

At three o'clock that afternoon a very elegant

young lady walked up the steps of the Settergreen home. It was Pippi Longstocking. For the sake of being different, her red hair was unbraided, and it fell about her like a lion's mane. She had painted her mouth a violent red with chalk, and blackened her eyebrows so much that she looked quite dangerous. With the red chalk she had also coloured all her nails, and she had put big green bows on her shoes.

'I should think I'll be the fanciest at *this* party,' she muttered, rather pleased with herself, as she rang the doorbell.

In the parlour of the Settergreen home sat three distinguished ladies, Tommy and Annika, and their mother. A splendidly laid table stood there, and a log-fire burned cheerily in the open fireplace. The ladies talked quietly with each other, and Tommy and Annika sat on the sofa and looked at an album. It was all very peaceful.

But suddenly the peace was broken.

'Attaaaaan-*shun*!'

A piercing cry came out of the front hall, and the next minute Pippi stood on the threshold. Her cry had been so loud and so unexpected that the ladies jumped in their seats.

'Company, forward M A R C H !' came the next cry, and Pippi went forward with measured steps to Mrs Settergreen.

'Company, H A L T !' She stopped.

'Present arms, one, T W O !' she yelled, taking Mrs Settergreen's hand in both of hers and shaking it heartily.

'Knees bend!' she cried, curtsying prettily. Then she leaned forward towards Mrs Settergreen and said in her usual voice, 'The fact of the matter is that I'm shy, so if I don't do this by commands, I'd just stand in the front hall and be contrary and not dare come in.'

Thereupon she rushed up to the other ladies and kissed them on the cheek.

'Charming, charming, upon my honour!' she said, for she had once heard a very fine gentleman say that to a lady. And then she sat down in the best chair she could see. Mrs Settergreen had thought that the children would have their party up in Tommy and Annika's room, but Pippi sat calmly where she was, slapped her knees, and said with her eyes on the tea-table, '*That* certainly looks good! When do we begin?'

At the same moment, Ella, the maid, came in with the teapot, and Mrs Settergreen said, 'Shall we have tea now?'

'Bags, I'm first!' shouted Pippi, and was at the table in two leaps. She scrambled together as many cakes as she could manage on one plate, slung five lumps of sugar into a teacup, emptied half the cream-pitcher into it as well, and returned to the chair with her plunder before the ladies had even come forward to the table.

Pippi stretched her legs out in front of her and put the plate of cakes between the tips of her toes. Then she plunged each cake with gusto into the teacup and pushed so much into her mouth that she couldn't get a word out, much as she tried. In a trice she had finished all the cakes on the plate. She stood up, hit on the plate like on a tambourine, and went up to the table to see if there were any left. The ladies looked disapprovingly at her, but she didn't notice that.

Gaily chattering, she went round the table and took a cake here and a cake there.

'It was really nice of you to invite me,' she said. 'I've never been to a tea party before.'

A big cream cake stood on the table. It was decorated with a red sweet in the middle. Pippi stood with her hands behind her back and looked at it. Suddenly, she bent down and snatched the sweet with her teeth. But she had bobbed a little too quickly, for when she came up again her whole face was a block of cream.

'Hahaha,' laughed Pippi. 'Now we can play blind-man's-buff, 'cause here we certainly have the blind-man free of charge. I can't see a thing!'

She stretched out her tongue and licked off all the cream.

'Well, it's terribly too bad about this,' she said. 'And the cake's quite ruined anyway, so it's just as well if I eat it up at once.'

And so she did. She went at it with a cake spade, and within a very short time, the whole cake had disappeared. Pippi rubbed her stomach with satisfaction. Mrs Settergreen had gone out to the kitchen for a moment and knew nothing of the accident with the cake. But the other ladies looked very sternly at Pippi. *They* would have liked some of that cake, too. Pippi noticed that they looked a bit dissatisfied, and she decided to cheer them up.

'Now, you mustn't be upset about such a little accident,' she said consolingly. 'The main thing is that we have our health. And at a tea party you ought to have fun.'

With these words she took the sugar-bowl from the table and sprinkled a good deal of sugar on the floor.

'Have you ever noticed what fun it is to walk on a floor that's got sugar on it?' she asked the ladies. 'It's even *more* fun, of course, going barefoot,' she continued, tearing off her shoes and stockings. 'I think you ought to try it too, 'cause there just isn't anything that feels better, you can take my word for that.'

But now Mrs Settergreen came in, and when she saw the spilled sugar she took Pippi firmly by the arm and led her over to Tommy and Annika on the sofa. Then she went and sat with the ladies and offered them another cup of tea. That the cake had disappeared only pleased her. She thought her guests had liked it so well they had eaten it all up.

Pippi, Tommy, and Annika talked quietly on the sofa, the fire crackled in the fireplace, the ladies drank their tea, and all was peace and quiet once again. As it now and then happens at tea parties, the ladies began talking about their maids. None of them seemed to have a particularly good one, for they were not at all satisfied and they agreed that the only solution was not to have a maid at all. It was far better to do everything oneself, for then at least one could be sure that it would be properly done.

Pippi sat on the sofa listening, and after a while she said, 'My grandmother once had a maid called Martha. She had chilblains on her feet, but otherwise there wasn't anything wrong with her. The only awkwardness was that as soon as strangers came she rushed forward and bit them in the leg. And scolded! Oh, how she scolded! You could hear it all over the neighbourhood. But it was only her way of being playful. The strangers didn't always understand that, though. There was an old vicar's wife who came to see grandmother once when Martha was new to her job. When Martha came running at her and sank her teeth into the lady's shin, she let out a howl which frightened Martha so much she bit her teeth together even harder, and then she couldn't get loose. She was stuck to the vicar's wife all the week till Friday. So grandmother had to peel the potatoes herself that day. But it got done properly, anyway. She peeled them so thoroughly that when she was finished there weren't any potatoes left. Just peel. After that Friday the vicar's wife never visited grandmother any more. She couldn't take a joke. And Martha, who was so funny and cheerful! Though for all that, she could be quite touchy too, no doubt about that. Once when grandmother drove a fork in her ear she went and sulked all day long.'

Pippi looked around and gave a friendly laugh.

'Well, that was Martha, *that* was,' she said, twiddling her thumbs.

The ladies looked as if they hadn't heard anything. They continued to talk.

'If my Rosa were at least *clean* at her work,' said Mrs Bergen, 'I could possibly keep her on. But she's simply piggish.'

'Then you should have seen Martha,' Pippi chimed in. 'Martha was so filthy to the core, it was a fright to see, grandmother said. But it was all genuine washable dirt, to be sure. Once at a bazaar at the Ritz Hotel she got first prize for the mourning-borders round her nails. Nuisance and miseries, but that girl was grubby!'

'Can you imagine,' said Mrs Granberg, 'the other evening when my Britta was going out, she simply borrowed my blue silk dress without a word! Isn't that the limit?'

'Well, I should say,' said Pippi. 'She seems on the whole to be made in the same mould as Martha, I can tell that. Grandmother had a pink vest she liked an awful lot. The trouble was that Martha liked it too. Each morning grandmother and Martha had a row over who should have the vest. At last they agreed to have it every other day, so's it would be fair. But even then Martha was troublesome! Sometimes she would come running in when it wasn't her turn at *all* and say, "Here! There'll be no mashed turnip served today if I can't have the pink wool vest!" Well now, what was grandmother to do? Mashed turnip was her favourite dish. Martha got the vest! And when she'd got it, she went out to the kitchen as sweet as could be and set to beating the mashed turnip so's it splashed on the walls.'

There was a moment's silence. Then Mrs Alexanderson said, 'Now, I'm not absolutely certain, but I strongly suspect that my Hilda steals. I *know* that things have been disappearing.'

'Martha . . . ' began Pippi, but Mrs Settergreen said firmly:

'The children may go upstairs immediately!'

'Yes—but, I was just going to tell how Martha stole too,' said Pippi. 'Like a magpie! Thick and fast! She used to get up in the middle of the night and steal a thing or two 'cause otherwise she couldn't sleep well, she said. Once she pinched grandmother's piano and jammed it in the top drawer of her bureau. She was very light-fingered, grandmother said.'

Now Tommy and Annika took Pippi by the arms and pulled her up the stairs. The ladies drank still more tea, and Mrs Settergreen said, 'I shouldn't really complain about my Ella, but she *does* break a great deal of china.'

A red head appeared at the top of the stairs.

'Speaking of Martha,' said Pippi, 'perhaps you're wondering if *she* used to break any china. Well, I should say she did! She had picked a special day of the week for it. It was on Tuesdays, grandmother said. And already about five o'clock on Tuesday mornings you could hear that brick of a girl smashing china in the kitchen. She began with cups and glasses and other light things, and went on later to those deep plates, and then the flat ones, and ended up with the platters. There was just one crash in the kitchen the whole morning, so *that* was a blessing, grandmother used to say. If Martha had some extra time in the afternoon, she'd go into the parlour with a little hammer and knock down all the antique East Indian plates that hung on the walls. Grandmother bought new china on Wednesdays,' said Pippi, disappearing up the stairs like a jack-in-the-box.

Now Mrs Settergreen's patience had come to an end. She ran up the stairs, into the children's room and up to Pippi, who had just begun teaching Tommy how to stand on his head.

'You may never come here again,' said Mrs Settergreen, 'since you behave so badly.'

Pippi looked at her with surprise, and her eyes slowly filled with tears.

'Well, that's that. I might have known I couldn't behave myself!' she said. 'There's no use trying. I just never will learn how. I should have stayed at sea.'

Then she curtsied to Mrs Settergreen, said goodbye to Tommy and Annika, and walked slowly down the stairs.

But now the ladies were also leaving. Pippi sat down by the umbrella stand in the front hall and looked at them while they put on their hats and coats.

'It's a pity you don't like your maids,' she said. 'You ought to have someone like Martha! A better girl you'll never find, grandmother always used to say. Just think, once at Christmas-time when Martha was going to serve the whole roasted pig, can you imagine what she did? She'd read in a cookery book that the Christmas pig should be served with curled paper and an apple in the mouth. Poor Martha didn't understand that it was the *pig* that should have the apple. You should have seen her when she came in on Christmas Eve, dressed in a starched white apron and with a big red Pippin in her mouth. Grandmother said to her, "You are a *nut*, Martha!" and 'course Martha couldn't get a word out for an answer. She just wiggled her ears so the paper rustled. She was trying to say something, but it just became "Blubb, blubb, blubb". 'Course, she couldn't bite people in the leg as she was used to doing, either, and just when there were so many strangers coming! No, there wasn't much fun for poor little Martha *that* Christmas Eve,' said Pippi sadly.

The ladies now had their street-clothes on, and so they said a last goodbye to Mrs Settergreen. And Pippi ran up to her and whispered, 'I'm sorry I couldn't behave myself. Goodbye!'

Then she slung on her big hat and followed the ladies out. Their ways separated outside. Pippi went towards Villekulla Cottage, and the ladies in the opposite direction.

When they had gone a little way, they heard something panting behind them. Pippi came bolting up to them.

'You can bet grandmother missed Martha when she lost her. Imagine, one Tuesday morning when Martha hadn't broken more than a dozen teacups, she went her way and took to the sea. So grandmother had to break the china herself that day. And she wasn't used to it, poor thing, so she got blisters on her hands. She never saw Martha again. And that was a shame, what with such a first-rate girl, grandmother said.'

Then Pippi went, and the ladies hurried on. But when they had gone a few hundred yards they heard Pippi from far off shouting with all her might:

'S-h-e n-e-v-e-r s-w-e-p-t u-n-d-e-r t-h-e b-e-d-s, M-a-r-t-h-a!'

10
Pippi Becomes a Heroine

One Sunday afternoon Pippi sat wondering what to do. Tommy and Annika were with their father and mother, who had been invited out to tea, so she couldn't expect a visit from them.

The day had been full of pleasant things to do. She had got up early and served Mr Nelson fruit juice and buns in bed. He had looked such a dear, sitting there in his light blue night-shirt holding the glass with both hands. Then she had fed and combed the horse and told him a long story about her travels on the seas. After that, she had gone into the parlour and done a big painting on the wall. It was a picture of a fat lady in a red dress and a black hat. In one hand she held a yellow flower and in the other a dead mouse. It was a very beautiful painting, Pippi thought; it brightened up the whole room. After that, she sat down by her cupboard and looked at all her birds' eggs and shells, and then she had remembered all the wonderful places where she and her father had gathered them together, and all the pleasant little shops the world over where they had bought all the fine things that were now kept in the drawers of her cupboard. After that, she had tried to teach Mr Nelson the polka, but he hadn't wanted to learn. For a moment she had thought of trying it with the horse, but instead she crawled into the woodbox and closed the lid over herself. She pretended that she was a sardine in a tin, and it was such a pity that Tommy and Annika weren't there or they could have been sardines too.

But now it began to get dark. Pippi pressed her little potato-nose against the window pane and looked out at the autumn twilight. Then she remembered that she hadn't ridden for several days, so she decided to do so right away. It would be a nice ending to a pleasant Sunday.

So she went and put on her big hat, fetched Mr Nelson, who was sitting in a corner playing with some marbles, saddled the horse, and lifted him down from the front porch. And off they rode, Mr Nelson sitting on Pippi, and Pippi sitting on the horse.

It was so cold the roads were frozen, and there was a loud clatter as they rode along. Mr Nelson sat on Pippi's shoulder and tried to catch hold of branches as they passed them, but Pippi rode so fast he couldn't. Instead, he got a good many cracks on his ears from the whizzing-by branches, and he had a hard time keeping his straw hat in place. Pippi rode through the little town, and the alarmed people pressed themselves as close as they could against the walls of the houses as she stormed by.

All Swedish country towns have a market place, and this town had one too. Around it stood the little town hall, which was painted yellow, and several beautiful single-storeyed houses. There was one rickety big building too. It was a newly-built three-storey house which was called the Skyscraper because it was taller than any of the other buildings in the town.

On this Sunday evening, the little town seemed a very still and peaceful place. But suddenly the peace was broken by a loud cry:

'The Skyscraper's burning! Fire! Fire!'

From all directions people came running with wide open eyes. A fire-engine drove through the streets with a terrible clanging, and the little children of the town, who had always thought it such fun to see the fire-engine before, were now so frightened they began to cry because they were sure that *their* houses were going to catch fire too. The square in front of the Skyscraper was filled with people. The police tried to keep them out of the way so that the fire-engine would be able to get through.

From the windows of the Skyscraper leaping flames forced their way, and smoke and sparks surrounded the firemen who bravely set about putting the fire out.

The fire had started in the ground floor, but spread quickly to the upper floors. Suddenly the people who stood gathered in the square saw a sight which made them gasp with horror. At the very top of the house there was an attic, and at the attic window, which had just been opened by a little child's hand, stood two small boys yelling for help.

'We can't come down 'cause somebody's made a fire in the stairs!' cried the bigger.

He was just five years old, and his brother was a year younger. Their mother had gone out on an errand, and now they stood there completely alone. Many people down in the square began to weep, and the head of the fire brigade looked anxious. Of course there was a ladder on the fire-engine, but it wasn't nearly long enough to reach so high up. And it was impossible to go into the house to rescue the children. The people in the square despaired when they realized the children could not be helped. And the poor little things just stood up there and cried. It wouldn't be many minutes before the fire would reach the attic too.

Pippi sat on her horse right in the middle of the crowd in the square. She looked with interest at the fire-engine, and wondered if she ought to buy herself one like it. She liked it because it was red, and because it had made so much noise driving through the streets. Then she looked at the crackling fire, and she thought it was fun when some sparks fell on her.

By and by she noticed the little boys in the attic. To her surprise they didn't seem to be enjoying the fire at all. It was more than she could understand, and finally she just had to ask those standing around her, 'Why are the children crying?'

At first she only got sobs for an answer, but then a fat man said, 'Why d'you suppose? Don't you think *you'd* cry if you were up there and couldn't come down?'

'I never cry,' said Pippi. 'But now, if they really want to come down, why is it nobody is helping them?'

'Because it can't be done, that's why,' said the fat man. Pippi thought for a moment.

'Could someone bring a long rope here?' she said.

'What good would that do?' said the fat man. 'The children are too small to climb down a rope. And for that matter, how would you get the rope up to them?'

'Oh, one learns things at sea,' said Pippi easily. 'I need a rope.'

Nobody believed that it would do any good, but somehow Pippi got a rope anyway.

A high tree grew by the Skyscraper's gable. The top of the tree was just about the same height as the attic window, but the distance between them was at least ten feet. The tree trunk was smooth and without a single branch on which to climb. Not even Pippi could have climbed it.

The fire burned, the children in the attic cried, and the people in the square wept.

Pippi climbed off her horse and went up to the tree. Then she took the rope and tied it to Mr Nelson's tail.

'Now, you're going to be Pippi's good boy, aren't you?' she said. Then she put him on the tree trunk and gave him a little push. He understood very well what he was supposed to do, and he obediently climbed up the tree. It was no trick at all for a little monkey to do that.

The people in the square held their breath and watched Mr Nelson. He soon reached the top of the tree. There he sat on a branch and looked down at Pippi. She waved at him to come down again, and he did so. But he climbed down on the other side of the branch, so that when he reached the ground again, the rope lay across the branch and hung down double with both ends on the ground.

'Mr Nelson, how clever you are! You could be a professor any old time,' said Pippi, undoing the knot that held one end of the rope to the little monkey's tail.

Close by, there was a house under repair. Pippi ran there and fetched a long plank. She held it under her arm, grabbed hold of the rope with her free hand, and then kicked against the tree with her feet. Quickly and easily she climbed up the rope, and the people stopped weeping out of sheer astonishment. When she had reached the top, she laid the plank across a heavy branch and pushed it carefully over to the attic window. The plank lay like a bridge between the top of the tree and the window.

The people in the square watched in silence. The suspense was so great, nobody could say a word. Pippi climbed out on the plank. She smiled in a friendly way at the boys in the attic.

'You're looking a bit unhappy,' said she. 'Have you got tummy-aches?'

She ran over the plank and hopped into the attic.

'It seems rather warm in here,' she said. 'You won't need to burn anything more today, that I can guarantee. And at the most, a very small fire in the grate tomorrow, I should think.'

Then she took a boy under each arm and climbed out on the plank again.

'Now you're really going to have a bit of fun,' she said. 'This is almost like tightrope walking.'

And when she had come to the middle of the plank, she lifted one leg straight into the air just as she had done in the circus. A murmur went through the crowd, and when Pippi lost one of her shoes a moment later, several old ladies fainted. But Pippi arrived safe and sound at the tree with the boys, and the crowd cheered so that their cheers rang out in the dark evening and drowned the crackling of the fire.

Then Pippi pulled the rope up to her and fastened one end firmly to a branch. To the other end of the rope she tied one of the boys, and then slowly and carefully lowered him to his overjoyed mother, who stood waiting in the square. With tears in her eyes, she threw her arms about her boy. But Pippi shouted, 'Untie the rope, can't you? There's still another one here, and he can't fly either.'

Some of the people helped to untie the knot and free the boy. Pippi really *could* tie knots! She'd learned that at sea. Then she pulled the rope up again, and it was the other boy's turn to be lowered.

Now Pippi alone was left in the tree. She jumped out on the plank, and all the people looked at her and wondered what she was about to do. Pippi danced back and forth on the narrow plank. She raised and lowered her arms delicately and sang in a hoarse voice which could barely be heard by the people in the square:

> 'A fire is burning,
> The flames are high,
> Oh, a fire is burning bright!
> It's burning for you,
> And it's burning for me,
> And for all who dance in the night!'

As she sang, she danced more and more wildly, and many of the people in the square shut their eyes with fright, for they were sure she would fall and hurt herself. Big flames curled out through the attic window, and they could see Pippi clearly in the glow from the fire. She raised her arms to the evening sky, and as a rain of sparks fell over her, she shouted, 'What a lovely, lovely, lovely fire!' Then she leaped right on to the rope.

'Wheee!' she cried, and slipped to the ground with the speed of greased lightning.

'Three cheers for Pippi Longstocking!' cried the head of the fire brigade.

'Hurrah! Hurrah! Hurrah!' the crowd shouted. But there was one who cheered *four* times. And that was Pippi.

11
Pippi Celebrates her Birthday

One day Tommy and Annika found a letter in their letterbox.

'TO TMMY AN ANIKA' it read on the outside. When they opened it, they found a card on which was written:

'TMMY AN ANIKA WIL KUM TO PIPPI FOR A BIRDAYPARTI TOMORRO AFTERNUN. DRESS: WAT YU PLEEZ.'

Tommy and Annika were so pleased, they began to hop and dance. They understood everything that was written on the card even though the spelling was a bit odd. Pippi had had fearful trouble in writing it. It is true that she hadn't known the letter 'i' the day she had been at school, but actually she could write just a little. During the time she had been at sea, one of the sailors on her father's boat had sometimes sat with her on the quarterdeck in the evenings and tried to teach her to write. Unfortunately, Pippi was not a very patient pupil. Quite suddenly she would say:

'No, Fridolf (for Fridolf was the name of the sailor), no, Fridolf, I don't give a fig for this. I'm going to climb to the top of the mast and take a look at what kind of weather we're having tomorrow.'

So it was no wonder that writing was a task for her. For a whole night she had sat and struggled with the invitation, and when the small hours of morning had come, and the stars were fading over the roof of Villekulla Cottage, she had trudged over to Tommy and Annika's house and stuffed the letter down in their letterbox.

As soon as Tommy and Annika came home from school, they began to dress for the party. Annika asked her mother to curl her hair, which she did. She tied a big pink ribbon in it too. Tommy combed his hair with water to make it lie really flat. *He* didn't have any use for curls and things! Annika wanted to put on her very best dress, but her mother said that it wasn't worthwhile, since Annika was seldom very clean and neat when she came home from Pippi; so Annika had to be satisfied with her next-best. Tommy didn't much care what he wore, as long as it was nice.

Of course they had bought a present for Pippi. They had taken the money out of their own piggy-banks, and on their way home from school they had run into the toyshop in the High Street and bought a *very* fine . . . well, just what it was can be a secret for a while. Now the present lay wrapped in green paper with lots of string round it. When Tommy and Annika were ready, Tommy took the package and they trotted away, followed by mother's anxious warnings to take care of their clothes. Annika was to carry the package for a while too, and they had agreed that when they presented it they should *both* hold it.

It was now well into November, and twilight came early. When Tommy and Annika went in through the gate of Villekulla Cottage, they held hands tightly, for it was just about dark in Pippi's orchard. The old trees, which were losing their last leaves, sighed and murmured gloomily in the wind. 'It's really autumn,' said Tommy. It was much more pleasant to see the lights shining in

Villekulla Cottage, and to know that a birthday party waited inside.

Usually Tommy and Annika scampered in the back way, but today they went to the front door. No horse was to be seen on the front porch. Tommy knocked politely on the door. From inside came a hollow voice:

'O, who comes through this cold, dark night
To knock on the door of my house?
Is it a ghost, or only just
A poor bedraggled mouse?'

'No, Pippi, it's us!' cried Annika. 'Open the door!'

Pippi opened it.

'Oh, Pippi, why did you say that about "ghost"? I got so scared!' said Annika, quite forgetting to congratulate Pippi.

Pippi laughed heartily and opened the door to the kitchen. How good it was to come into the light and warmth! The birthday party was to be held in the kitchen, for it was cosiest there. There were only two other rooms on the lower floor. One was the parlour, which had only one piece of furniture, and the other was Pippi's bedroom. But the kitchen was big and roomy, and Pippi had prettied it up and made it tidy. She had put rugs on the floor, and on the table lay a new cloth which she had sewn herself. The flowers which she had embroidered on it *did* look a bit odd, but Pippi said that such flowers grew in Indo-China, and so everything was as it should be. The curtains were drawn, and in the grate a fire burned and the sparks flew. Mr Nelson sat on the wood box hitting two saucepan-lids together, and in a far corner stood the horse. Naturally, he had been invited to the party as well.

Now at last Tommy and Annika remembered that they should congratulate Pippi. Tommy bowed and Annika curtsied, and then they held the green package forward and said, 'Many happy returns of the day!' Pippi thanked them and eagerly tore open the package. And there lay a musical box! Pippi became quite wild with delight. She hugged Tommy, and she hugged Annika, and she hugged the musical box, and she hugged the paper in which it had been wrapped. Then she turned the handle of the musical box, and with many a plink and a plonk, a melody which was supposed to be 'The More We are Together' came forth.

Pippi turned the handle round and round, and forgot all else. But suddenly she remembered something.

'Dear hearts!' she said. 'You must have *your* birthday presents too!'

'But it isn't our birthday today,' said Annika.

'No, but it's mine, so I should think I could give you birthday presents too. Or is it written somewhere in your lesson books that it can't be done? Does it have something to do with pluttification that makes it so's it can't be done?'

'No, of *course* it can be done,' said Tommy. 'Though it's not usual. But I'd *like* to have a present!'

'I, too!' said Annika.

Pippi ran into the parlour and fetched two packages which lay on the cupboard. When Tommy opened his package, he found a strange little ivory flute, and in Annika's package lay a beautiful brooch in the shape of a butterfly. The wings were set with red, blue, and green stones.

Now that everyone had a birthday present, it was time to sit down at the table. There were piles of cakes and buns waiting. The cakes had rather odd shapes, but Pippi said that they made cakes like that in China.

Pippi poured hot chocolate with whipped cream into the cups, and then they were ready to sit down. But Tommy said, 'When mother and father give a dinner, the gentlemen always get cards that say which lady they should take to the table. I think we should do that too.'

'Full speed ahead,' said Pippi.

'It won't be as good for us, though, since I'm the only gentleman,' said Tommy undecidedly.

'Nonsense,' said Pippi. 'Do you suppose Mr Nelson is a young lady then?'

'No, of course not! I forgot Mr Nelson,' said Tommy. And then he sat down on the wood box and wrote on a card:

'Mr Settergreen will have the pleasure of taking Miss Longstocking.'

'Mr Settergreen is me,' he said with satisfaction, showing the card to Pippi. Then he wrote on the next card:

'Mr Nelson will have the pleasure of taking Miss Settergreen.'

'Yes, but the horse has to have a card too,' said Pippi definitely. 'Even if he can't sit at the table!'

So as Pippi dictated, Tommy wrote on the next card:

'The horse will have the pleasure of staying put in the corner, then he will get cakes and sugar.'

Pippi held the card under the horse's nose and said, 'Read this, and tell me what you think!'

As the horse had no objections, Tommy offered Pippi his arm, and they went to the table. Mr Nelson made no effort to invite Annika, so she simply lifted him up and brought him along.

He refused to sit on a chair, but sat right on the table. He didn't want chocolate with whipped cream either, but when Pippi filled his cup with water, he held it with both hands and drank.

Annika and Tommy and Pippi tucked in, and Annika said that if these were the kind of cakes they had in China, then she was going to move to China when she grew up.

When Mr Nelson had emptied his cup, he turned it upside down and put it on his head. As soon as Pippi saw this she did the same but as she hadn't finished drinking all her chocolate, a little brown stream ran down her forehead and continued down her nose. Pippi stuck out her tongue and stopped it.

'Waste not, want not,' she said.

Tommy and Annika carefully licked out their cups before they put them on their heads.

When they were all quite full and satisfied, and the horse had been given what he was to have, Pippi promptly took hold of the four corners of the tablecloth and lifted it off so that cups and plates fell over each other as in a sack. She stuffed the whole bundle into the wood box.

'I always like tidying up a bit as soon as I've finished eating,' she said.

Then it was time to play. Pippi suggested they play a game called 'Don't Fall to the Floor'. It was very simple. All you had to do was crawl round the whole kitchen without once setting foot on the floor. Pippi shot around in one second. But it went quite well even for Tommy and Annika. You started with the kitchen sink and if you could stretch your legs wide enough, it was possible to come over to the open fireplace, and from there to the wood box, from the wood box over a shelf, and so down on to the table. From there you went over two chairs to the cupboard in the corner. Between the cupboard and the sink there was a distance of several yards, but there, luckily, stood the horse. If you climbed up on him at the tail end and slid off at the head end, and then jerked at just the right moment, you landed right on the draining board.

When they had played this a while, and Annika's dress was no longer her next-best, but only her next-next-next-best, and Tommy had become as black as a chimney sweep, they decided to think of something else to play.

'Let's go up to the attic and say hello to the ghosts,' suggested Pippi.

Annika gasped.

'A . . . a . . . are there *ghosts* in the attic?' she said.

'Are there! Lots of 'em,' said Pippi. 'It's crawling with different kinds of phantoms and ghosts up there. You stumble on them without any trouble. Do you want to go?'

'Oh,' said Annika, and looked reproachfully at Pippi.

'Mother says there aren't any ghosts or phantoms,' said Tommy boldly.

'That's quite true,' said Pippi. 'Any place but here, 'cause they live in my attic, all there are. It doesn't do any good to ask them to move. But they don't do any harm. They just pinch you on the arm so's it gets black and blue, and they *howl*. And play ninepins with their heads.'

'Th . . . th . . . they play ninepins with their *heads*?' whispered Annika.

'Just what they do,' said Pippi. 'Come on, let's go up and talk to them. I'm good at ninepins.'

Tommy didn't want to show he was afraid, and in a way he really *did* rather want to see a ghost. That would be something to tell the boys at school! Besides, he comforted himself with the thought that the ghosts would never dare to try anything with Pippi. He decided to go along. Poor Annika didn't want to at all, but she happened to think that possibly a tiny ghost might slip down to her while she was alone in the kitchen. That settled the matter! Better to be with Pippi and Tommy among a thousand ghosts than alone with even the tiniest little baby ghost in the kitchen!

Pippi went first. She opened the door to the attic. It was pitch dark. Tommy held on tightly to Pippi, and Annika held on even more tightly to Tommy. Then they went up the stairs, which creaked and groaned at every step. Tommy began to wonder if it would have been better to forget the whole thing, and Annika didn't need to wonder. She was quite sure of it.

By and by, they had reached the top of the stairs and were standing in the attic. It was completely dark there except for a narrow stream of moonlight which fell across the floor. There were sighs and whistles in every corner as the wind blew in through the cracks.

'Hail, all ghosts!' shouted Pippi.

But if there was a ghost there, he made no reply.

'Well, of course, I might have known,' said Pippi. 'They've gone to a committee meeting of the Society of Honourable Ghosts and Phantoms!'

A sigh of relief escaped from Annika, and she hoped that the committee meeting would last a long time. But just then a terrible cry came from one corner of the attic.

'Klaawitt,' it cried, and the next moment Tommy saw something whistling towards him in the dark. He felt it fan him on the forehead, and then something black disappeared through a little window which stood open. He yelled wildly, 'A ghost! A ghost!'

Annika joined in.

'That poor fellow's going to be late for the meeting,' said Pippi. 'If it *was* a ghost! And not an owl! Anyway, there aren't any ghosts,' she continued after a while, 'so the more I think about it, the more it was an owl. If anybody says there are ghosts, I'll tweak his nose!'

'But you said so yourself!' said Annika.

'Oh, I did, did I?' said Pippi. 'Well then, I'll certainly have to tweak my nose.'

And she took hold of her own nose and gave it a sharp twist.

After this Tommy and Annika felt a bit calmer. They were even so brave that they dared to go up to the window and look out over the orchard. Big, dark clouds drove across the sky and did their best to hide the moon. The trees bent and murmured.

Tommy and Annika turned about. But then— oh, so terrible!—they saw a white figure moving towards them.

'A ghost!' Tommy screamed wildly.

Annika was so frightened that she couldn't even scream. The figure came even closer. Tommy and Annika clung to each other and shut their eyes. Then they heard it say:

'Look what I've found! Father's nightshirt was in an old seaman's chest over here. If I turn it up round the bottom I can use it myself.'

Pippi came forward to them with the nightshirt dragging round her feet.

'Oh, Pippi, I could have died of fright!' said Annika.

'But there's nothing dangerous about nightshirts,' protested Pippi. 'They never bite, 'cept in self-defence.'

Pippi decided that this was the right time to go through the seaman's chest properly. She carried it up to the window and opened the lid so that the pale moonlight fell over the contents. There were a lot of old clothes, which she tossed on the floor, a telescope, a couple of old books, three pistols, a sword, and a bag of gold pieces.

'Tiddelipom and poddeliday,' said Pippi happily.

'How exciting!' said Tommy.

Pippi gathered everything together in the nightshirt, and they went down to the kitchen again. Annika was very happy to be out of the attic.

'Never let children handle firearms,' said Pippi, taking a pistol in each hand. 'Otherwise, an accident can easily happen.' And she fired both pistols at the same time. '*That* was a good-sized bang,' she announced, looking up at the ceiling.

There were two holes in it where the bullets had gone through.

'Who knows,' she said hopefully, 'perhaps the bullets have gone straight through the roof and hit some of those ghosts in the leg. *That* will teach them to think twice the next time they mean to go scaring little innocent children. 'Cause even if they don't exist, that's no excuse for scaring people out of their wits. Would you each like a pistol, by the way?' she asked.

Tommy was thrilled, and Annika said she would like a pistol too, if it weren't loaded.

'Now we can become a band of robbers if we want to,' said Pippi, looking through the telescope. 'I can almost see the fleas in South America with this thing, I think,' she continued. 'It will be a good thing to have if we form a band of robbers.'

Just then there was a knock at the door. It was Tommy's and Annika's father, who had come to take them home. It was long past bed-time, he declared. Tommy and Annika had to hurry with thanking and saying goodbye and gathering together their possessions, the flute and the brooch and the pistols.

Pippi followed her guests to the front porch and saw them disappear down the orchard path. They turned about and waved. The light from inside fell over Pippi. There she stood with her stiff red pigtails, her father's nightshirt dragging round her feet. She held a pistol in one hand, and in the other a sword. She was presenting arms with it.

When Tommy and Annika and their father reached the gate, they heard her shouting after them. They stopped and listened. The wind was howling through the trees so that her voice scarcely reached them. But they did hear her anyway.

'I'm going to be a pirate when I grow up,' she shouted. 'Are you?'

Other Oxford Children's Modern Classics

The Piemakers
Helen Cresswell
ISBN 0 19 271809 6

Arthy, Jem, and Gravella Roller are the finest pie-makers in
Danby Dale, famed for their perfect pastry and fantastic
fillings. So when they're asked to make a special pie for the
king, which will feed two hundred people, the Rollers are
thrown into a frenzy of excited preparations. This will be the
best ever Danby Dale pie! But unfortunately, wicked Uncle
Crispin, a rival pie-maker, has different plans for the Rollers'
pie . . . plans that include an extra-large helping of pepper . . .

This funny, charming story was Helen Cresswell's first
children's book, and was nominated for the Carnegie Medal.

The Ship That Flew
Hilda Lewis
ISBN 0 19 271768 5

Peter sees the model ship in the shop window and he wants it
more than anything else on earth. But it is no ordinary model.
The ship takes Peter and his brother and sisters on magical
flights, wherever they ask to go. They fly around the world
and back into the past. But how long can you keep a ship that
is worth everything in the world, and a bit over . . . ?

Tom's Midnight Garden
Philippa Pearce
ISBN 0 19 271793 6 (hardback)
ISBN 0 19 271777 4 (paperback)

Winner of the Carnegie Medal.

Tom has to spend the summer at his aunt's and it seems as if
nothing good will ever happen again. Then he hears the
grandfather clock strike thirteen—and everything changes.
Outside the door is a garden—a garden that shouldn't exist.
Are the children there ghosts—or is it Tom who is the ghost?

Minnow on the Say
Philippa Pearce
ISBN 0 19 271778 2

David couldn't believe his eyes. Wedged by the landing stage
at the bottom of the garden was a canoe. The *Minnow*. David
traces the canoe's owner, Adam, and they begin a summer of
adventures. The *Minnow* takes them on a treasure hunt along
the river. But they are not the only people looking for
treasure, and soon they are caught in a race against time . . .

A Little Lower than the Angels
Geraldine McCaughrean
ISBN 0 19 271780 4

Winner of the Whitbread Children's Novel Award

Gabriel has no idea what the future will hold when he runs
away from his apprenticeship with the bad-tempered
stonemason. But God Himself, in the shape of playmaster
Garvey, has plans for him. He wants Gabriel for his angel . . .
But will Gabriel's new life with the travelling players be any
more secure? In a world of illusion, people are not always what
they seem. Least of all Gabriel.

A Pack of Lies
Geraldine McCaughrean
ISBN 0 19 271788 X

Winner of the Carnegie Medal and the Guardian Children's
Fiction Award

Ailsa's life is turned upside down when a strange man moves
into her mother's antique shop. He keeps the customers
spellbound with his outrageous stories—adventure, horror,
romance, mystery—but Ailsa doesn't believe a word. It's all
just a pack of lies.

The Hounds of the Morrigan
Pat O'Shea
ISBN 0 19 271773 1

The Great Queen, the Morrigan, is coming from the West, bringing destruction to the world. Only two children can stop her. At times their task seems impossible, and danger is always present. But they are guided in their quest by an unforgettable collection of humorous and joyful characters.

But all the time the Morrigan's hounds are trailing them . . .

The Great Elephant Chase
Gillian Cross
ISBN 0 19 271786 3

Winner of The Smarties Prize and the Whitbread Children's Novel Award

The elephant changed their lives for ever. Because of the elephant, Tad and Cissie become entangled in a chase across America, by train, by flatboat and steam boat. Close behind is Hannibal Jackson, who is determined to have the elephant for himself. And how do you hide an enormous Indian elephant?

The Eagle of the Ninth
Rosemary Sutcliff
ISBN 0 19 271765 0

The Ninth Legion marched into the mists of northern Britain.
And they never came back. Four thousand men disappeared
and the Eagle standard was lost. Marcus Aquila, a young
Roman officer, needs to find out what happened to his father
and the Ninth Legion. He sets out into the unknown territory
of the north on a quest so hazardous that no one expects him
to return . . .

Outcast
Rosemary Sutcliff
ISBN 0 19 271766 9

Sickness and death came to the tribe. They said it was because
of Beric, because he had brought down the Anger of the
Gods. The warriors of the tribe cast him out. Alone without
friends, family or tribe, Beric faces the dangers of the Roman
world.

The Silver Branch
Rosemary Sutcliff
ISBN 0 19 271765 2

Violence and intrigue are undermining Rome's influence in
Britain. And in the middle of the unrest, Justin and Flavius
uncover a plot to overthrow the Emperor. In fear for their
lives, they find themselves leading a tattered band of loyalists
into the thick of battle in defence of the honour of Rome.

The Lantern Bearers
Rosemary Sutcliff
ISBN 0 19 271763 4

Winner of the Carnegie Medal

The last of the Roman army have set sail and left Britain for
ever. They have abandoned the country to civil war and the
threat of Saxon invasion. When his home and all he loves are
destroyed, Aquila fights to bring some meaning back into his
life, and with it the hope of revenge . . .